THE DEVIL'S P...

When bounty hunter John Harrison captures fugitive outlaw Clay Barton, he's persuaded by Maggie Sloane to allow the captive to lead them to the loot robbed from an army payroll. But Barton double-crosses them and the mysterious Leo Gabriel kidnaps Maggie. With a veteran Buffalo Soldier, Sergeant Eli Johnson, at his side, Harrison battles ruthless vaqueros and a Comanche war party to recover the money, re-capture Barton and rescue Maggie . . . but a surprise awaits him when he finally catches up with his enemies . . .

PAUL GREEN

THE DEVIL'S PAYROLL

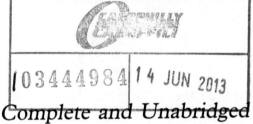

Complete and Unabridged

LINFORD
Leicester

First published in Great Britain in 2011 by
Robert Hale Limited
London

First Linford Edition
published 2013
by arrangement with
Robert Hale Limited
London

A catalogue record for this book is available
from the British Library.

ISBN 978–1–4448–1599–3

Published by
F. A. Thorpe (Publishing)
Anstey, Leicestershire

Set by Words & Graphics Ltd.
Anstey, Leicestershire
Printed and bound in Great Britain by
T. J. International Ltd., Padstow, Cornwall

This book is printed on acid-free paper

To my wife Emma, with love

1

The sun was reaching its zenith as John 'Gentleman Jack' Harrison rode into Brandon. Despite the scorching heat he wore a string tie and black frock-coat, for these were the clothes he was used to, just like the pearl-handled silver guns sitting snugly in each holster. Harrison held the reins lightly, his dark, hooded eyes scanning the dusty street. He slowed to a halt and removed his hat as a funeral procession passed by, the single mourner a striking red-haired woman who appeared dry-eyed and impassive as she walked behind the black carriage and plumed horses. Then, finding himself outside the town's hardware store, he dismounted and tethered his horse. Stepping inside, he inhaled the cooler air and smell of wood-shavings.

'Hot one, ain't it?' the storekeeper enquired as he looked up from his accounts.

'It certainly is.' He withdrew the poster he carried with him from inside his coat and unfolded it on the counter between them. 'Have you seen this man around these parts?'

The storekeeper looked at the drawing of Clay Barton below the words WANTED FOR MURDER DEAD OR ALIVE. $1000 REWARD and studied the well-dressed stranger more closely. This time he noticed the distinctive guns, while recalling that high-class drawl.

'Say, mister, haven't I read about you someplace?'

Harrison sighed. The dime novel, telling exaggerated tales of his exploits, had apparently sold well but fame was a hindrance to a bounty hunter. He might need to rely on the element of surprise. 'I'm sure you have but I wouldn't believe a word of it if I were you.'

Looking again at the poster the old man nodded slowly. 'That fella was here sure enough but he hightailed it after that shootin' a couple of days back. Seems he ran into a man he owed

2

money to who drew on 'im when he wouldn't pay up. Your man drew faster but then left pretty quick.'

Harrison jerked his head towards the window. 'Is that why there's a funeral out there?'

The storekeeper grinned. 'Pretty little thing, eh? I wouldn't go gettin' meself all shot up if I had her to warm the bed!'

Harrison smiled in response. 'Do you have any idea where Barton went?'

The storekeeper shrugged. 'Looked like he was ridin' south but there's not much between here and the Mexican border except Comanche, bandits and a few desert towns.' He paused for a moment, and then raised a crooked finger. 'Nearest place is called Blue Water Spring, 'bout half a day's ride from here. It's nothin' but a one horse town with a waterin' hole and a whorehouse that calls itself a hotel.'

He could reach that by nightfall. For a man on the run like Barton it might be a place to hide and rest up a while before making for the border. 'Much obliged to you,' Harrison said as he turned and headed for the door.

'Wait up, mister!' With surprising agility the stooped, elderly storekeeper scuttled from behind the counter and was at his side, the gaudy cover of *Gentleman Jack, Scourge of the Outlaw* by George Barrett visible in his gnarled hands. 'C'mon, tell me afore ya go. Did you really do all them things it says in this here book?'

'I'm afraid that Mr Barrett has a rather vivid imagination. I'll shoot a man when I have to but only if he draws on me first. I've put an end to a few bank robbers but I'm no gunslinger,' said Harrison drily. 'As for the rest, I'm just a lonely widower and if the ladies swoon over me, I certainly haven't noticed it. Does that answer your question?'

The storekeeper mumbled his sympathies as he looked sheepishly at the floor, but Harrison was already outside, mounting his chestnut mare. The cemetery was at the end of town and the formalities had just been completed as he rode past.

Slowing to a halt, he spied the widow leaving by the gate. 'Pardon me, ma'am,' he said as he raised his hat. She turned to face him and Harrison found himself gazing into a pair of wide ocean blue eyes. He hesitated briefly, his speech somehow arrested by their cool depths.

'I'm John Harrison. The man who shot your husband was a cold blooded killer. He murdered a guard while escaping from prison in Arizona and I hope it will give you some comfort when I bring him to justice.'

The woman smiled wryly. 'I see. Is justice your only reward, Mr Harrison?'

He stiffened slightly in the saddle. 'It's true I'll get paid a thousand dollars but I only go after the worst killers.'

Her smile vanished. 'Well, my husband got a bullet in the gut and I didn't even get what he was owed to bury him with, never mind no thousand dollars. I used my savings to give him the best farewell I could.'

Harrison felt suddenly chastened by her remarks. 'What was your husband called?' he asked.

'Joel Sloane. I'm Maggie Sloane by the way.'

'Well, Mrs Sloane, I'll see that a hundred dollars of that reward money goes to settle your costs. Would that help?'

The smile she gave him then would have melted the heart of Lucifer himself. 'That sounds like the sort of offer only Gentleman Jack could make. Here's my hand on it.'

He gently kissed her gloved fingers. 'I'm cut from the same crooked timber as everyone else, Mrs Sloane. Don't let any dime novel convince you otherwise.' With that he was gone.

The heat of the day burned itself out against an orange-red sunset as Harrison rode into Blue Water Spring. Raucous laughter and the tinkling sound of a piano guided him towards a clapboard house, painted gaudily in red.

As he tended his horse in the stable at the side he noticed a pinto slumbering in the next stall, which fitted the description of the one Barton was riding when he was last seen. The battered sign at the front above the swing back doors creaked in the breeze and he saw the words JACKSON'S HOTEL. The mingled smells of stale liquor, cigar smoke and cheap perfume assaulted his nostrils as he stepped inside. Beyond the crowded saloon bar a staircase covered by a threadbare carpet led to the rooms upstairs. Amid the noise and smoke his entry was barely noticed and there, in a far corner of the room, lounged Clay Barton. The gaunt, unshaven features, disfigured by a jagged scar down the right cheek, tousled jet-black hair and narrow eyes swam clearly into focus as Harrison stepped nearer. Barton's attention was clearly drawn to his blonde companion's cleavage and he did not appear to notice that he was being watched.

Turning to his left, he called the bartender over and ordered a whiskey. 'Do you have a room for tonight?' he asked.

The man grinned, showing broken teeth. 'Sure. Anything else you want?'

Harrison threw some silver dollars down on the bar 'A hot steak sent up to the best room you've got, the rest of that bottle and some information.'

'First two no problem, but the third . . . ' The man shrugged. 'That might cost more.'

Harrison tossed a few notes from his billfold towards the man. 'Tell me about Scarface in the corner over there. What room is he in?'

'Number four, you'll be a coupla doors down. He run off with your woman or somethin'?'

'I'm paying so I'll ask the questions, but not a word to Scarface, understand?'

'Take it easy, mister, tombstones talk more than I do,' said the bartender as he handed Harrison the key to room six.

He had drunk nearly half the bottle before the steak arrived, brought up with potatoes and a pot of coffee by a young girl who was clearly disappointed when Harrison showed no interest in her services. The meat was tough, with some gristle, but he was hungry and wolfed it down before sloshing more whiskey into a cup of tepid coffee. It did not stop the nightmares though, beginning with that frantic ride back to Richmond after he had deserted his post upon seeing the flames.

All was as it had been on that night until he reached what had once been his home. Instead of the blackened ruin he had encountered then, this time the house was still burning, engulfed by flames. He saw their screaming faces at the window before Elizabeth and Annie caught fire, the glass shattered and they fell towards him like human torches and he smelled their burning flesh.

He awoke drenched in sweat, his mouth dry and his head heavy. Cursing, he got up and staggered over to the tin bath which the girl had filled for him hours before. Harrison gasped as he plunged into the now cold water, submerging his body. He soaped himself, washed off and dried his aching limbs with the frayed towel. Once dressed he felt better and he made his way to Barton's room as dawn broke, dismissing the horrors of the previous night, as he habitually did, to concentrate on the job in hand.

Harrison turned the knob slowly and found the door unlocked. Stepping inside he aimed his gun at the figure huddled under the bedclothes. 'Time to wake up, Barton.'

The blonde girl he had seen the previous night sat up and winked at him, the sheet barely covering her ample breasts. At the same moment hard metal prodded his ribs. 'Drop the gun on the bed, mister, real slow.' He obeyed the rasping voice and the other pistol was removed quickly from its holster and tossed in the same direction.

'Throw 'em outside, Becky.' The girl slid from the bed without bothering to cover her nakedness and dropped the weapons out of a window facing the street. She then stooped to pull on a purple dress, winking again at him as she did so.

'You won't get far, Barton. There's a posse out looking for you.'

He heard the killer snort contemptuously behind him. 'Nobody in these parts cares about some dumb prison guard from Tucson. Now move, we're goin' downstairs.'

Barton directed him through a back exit to the stables, Becky following behind. Harrison was told to halt and turn around under a cross-beam. Without taking his eyes off his prisoner, the outlaw took a length of rope hanging from a nail in the wall and tossed it over to the girl. 'Tie one end over that beam, honey. There's a stool there you can stand on.'

Barton grinned wolfishly. 'See, I got it all figured out. I plan the same end for you as you did for me. Becky here's a real live guardian angel, been findin' out from her friends here if anyone's come lookin' for me.'

'You never said nothin' about no killin', Clay,' said the girl nervously. 'I might lie on my back for dollars but I ain't never killed.'

Seeing his chance, Harrison said, 'If you do what he says you'll be guilty of murder. That pretty neck of yours could get stretched too.'

'You shuddup!' Enraged at the prospect of having to merely shoot his enemy, Barton turned to the girl. 'Do like I tell ya or you won't get a cent!'

The moment of distraction was enough for Harrison and he launched himself at his adversary, jerking the other man's arm upwards as they crashed to the ground. The girl screamed and horses whinnied as Barton's gun fired twice before Harrison bashed his opponent's fist against a nearby post, sending the weapon spinning across the floor.

Barton's boot lashed out as he shouted in pain and Harrison staggered back, winded. He dodged the next blow as both men jumped to their feet but

Barton grabbed a pitchfork and lunged viciously at him. The prongs stuck in the wall, splintering wood as Harrison twisted to one side. Abandoning his now useless weapon, Barton came at him with a punch to the jaw that sent him sprawling, but he rolled aside quickly, grabbed the man's foot as he tried to stamp on his head and twisted hard. Harrison was on his feet as his opponent fell, punched him hard as he tried to get up and then brought his knee up into the fugitive's groin. He stepped back as Barton charged at him like an enraged bull and clipped him neatly under the jaw. As he fell once more the outlaw's head struck the edge of a water trough, and he lay still in a crumpled heap on the floor.

Becky stood cowering in a corner and Harrison told her, 'No one's going to hurt you, it's all right.' He turned back to his prisoner breathing heavily from his exertions, as the girl fled. Within minutes, he had Barton tied on to the pinto, had retrieved his guns from the street and was heading out into the desert, whistling softly as he left Blue Water Spring behind him.

It was not long before his prisoner stirred and, groaning as he sat upright, asked for water. Harrison held the bottle up to Barton's parched lips and the man drank greedily.

'If a man's gonna hang I figure he's a right to know who's doin' the hangin'. What's your name?'

'I'm John Harrison but it's the judge who'll sentence you, not me. Besides, you put a rope around your own neck when you shot that guard.'

Barton smiled. 'That how you square your conscience, Harrison? Tell me, how much will you get for this job?'

'A thousand dollars, all clean money and stolen from no one.'

Barton chuckled, despite his predicament. 'Ain't no such thing as clean money. Anyhow, it all adds up to the years you're stealin' from another man's life.'

Harrison said nothing but got back on his own horse, jerked the rope which

14

tied Barton's mount to his and set off once more. His prisoner was keen to continue talking however.

'Say, Harrison, how'd you like me to cut you in on a deal?'

Now it was Harrison's turn to laugh. 'You're hardly in a position to bargain.'

'Well, that's where you're wrong, see. D'you know why I was in prison? Me and a gang o' fellas robbed an army payroll. Hell, during the war I robbed banks for the Confederacy, so when we lost I figured I might as well steal for myself. Anyway, we all got shot up pretty bad but I escaped with this scar and a strongbox full o' money and buried it near the border. Carryin' it was slowin' me up some and I figured I'd get caught if I didn't hide it some place, then come back when it was safe.'

'Let me guess. You got caught after you'd buried it and were on your way to collect when, unfortunately, I showed up?'

'That's the truth. I ran into a posse just as I was about to cross over into

Mexico where the law can't touch me. And you know what, I'm the only man alive who knows where that money is. Cut me loose and we're partners. Fifty-fifty split. I don't rightly know how much there is in that box but it's at least a hundred times what you'll get for my neck.'

Harrison shook his head. 'Even if I believed your story, Barton, how could I trust you? You'd slit my throat while I slept, steal my horse and then just dig up the loot by yourself. Besides, Comanches raid that border area and there are bandits rustling cattle who'll shoot a man as soon as look at him.'

'Then leave me tied up all the way. I don't blame you for not trusting me, but the money's there. It's a lotta money and worth the risk for men who know their way around. Get rich or die tryin', that's what I say.'

There was a wheedling, anxious tone to Barton's voice. Was he telling the truth? Or was this the ploy of a man desperate to cheat the hangman's noose, hoping to buy a little more time? Harrison decided to change the subject for a while. 'Tell me, did you ever borrow money from anyone on the strength of that story?'

'I've never told anyone else about that money, never!'

'Then what about Joel Sloane, the man you shot in Brandon? I heard he drew on you after you refused to pay back the money you owed him.'

They had just entered a steep canyon and Barton's reply died on his lips as three horsemen approached, blocking the narrow path ahead. They were all Mexican; the one in the middle held the reins of a white mare in one hand and a pistol in the other. He leaned forward in the saddle as they all came to a halt and pushed his sombrero back to reveal a fleshy, bearded face in which a wall eye was the most prominent feature.

'I don't want any trouble,' said Harrison.

The bearded man responded with a belly laugh which echoed around the canyon. Turning to the man on his left he said 'How about that, Miguel? The man say he want no trouble, yet he tie his friend up like that.' Shaking his head, he tutted in mock disapproval. 'Well, we don't want no trouble neither. We just want your horses and any money you got.'

Miguel giggled as he added, 'If they got plenty money, maybe we not kill them eh, Sancho?'

Barton cut in. 'Listen, I'm a wanted man, so if you let me throw in my lot with you — '

Sancho kept his eyes on Harrison as he cocked his gun. 'Enough words, gringos!' He gestured for Harrison to dismount. 'Don't make me wait too long,' he said.

'Look, my prisoner's worth a lot more to you than the horses or anything in the saddle-bags. If I prove it to you will you let me go?' asked Harrison.

'Go on,' said Sancho as his one good eye narrowed suspiciously.

'There's something to show you in my inside pocket. If I move slowly, can I get it?'

'No tricks,' said the Mexican with a nod, raising his gun slightly.

Harrison drew out the Wanted poster and handed it across. Sancho grinned as he scanned the contents and his companions leaned towards him. The split second in which they were distracted was long enough. Both guns slid from Harrison's holsters and were fired in what seemed like one fluid movement as the first bullet went straight through Sancho's heart. Miguel was reaching for his weapon when the second ripped into his lungs. The third man fired harmlessly into the air as two more bullets hit him squarely in the chest.

Barton shook his head in amazement. 'Never would have figured that,' he remarked as Harrison dismounted in time to stop Miguel from reaching for the gun that lay nearest him. He placed his boot firmly on the barrel of the dying bandit's weapon as he bent down to give him some water.

'I'm sorry you're going to die, son,

but you intended to kill me. Now, the rest of your outfit, where are they?' Miguel shook his head weakly. Blood was coughed up from his lungs as he tried to say something, then he stiffened and lay still.

'Damn, there could be more of them,' muttered Harrison as he straightened up. He was aware of someone behind him just as the sound of a rifle being fired at close range echoed around the canyon. He froze, expecting the burning pain of a fatal wound before a fall into oblivion, but then he realized that he had not been hit. Turning slowly, Harrison found himself staring at the body of another dead bandit who had just been shot in the back. He looked up and into the eyes of the owner of the still smoking gun. Though dressed in a buffalo jacket and pants, with her hair tied under a wide-brimmed hat, he would have recognized her anywhere. It was Maggie Sloane.

2

Harrison tipped his hat. 'I've no idea why you're here but I'm obliged, ma'am.'

The widow shrugged. 'I've been tracking you since you left Brandon. My father was an army scout so I guess it must be in the blood.' Then she turned her rifle towards Barton.

'Clay Barton, if you don't lead me to Joel's money I swear I'll blast you to hell!'

'It ain't Joel's money. Sure, he thought the plan up but he weren't riskin' his neck to steal it!' Barton's tone was defiant but the sweat above his trembling lip betrayed his fear.

'So that's why your husband was shot, the usual dishonour among thieves,' said Harrison drily.

Maggie turned back to him, her eyes blazing. 'Joel was just an army stores clerk who did what the officers told him. They made sure he was the one to take the blame when it turned out money was being skimmed off the contracts. When he realized that he was going to be kicked out and lose his pension, that's when he used what he knew to get us set up for life.' She jerked her head in Barton's direction. 'It all went wrong, of course, and now he's the only one who knows where there's any money.'

'Barton's wanted for murder, Mrs Sloane and he killed your husband. All the money in the world won't change that.'

'Maybe not but it'll put food on the table and give my two young boys a better chance in life. That's how Clay Barton can make amends for what he's done.' Sensing Harrison's hesitation, she moved closer to place a hand on his arm.

'Please, I'm begging you, Mr Harrison. Didn't we all see enough killing in the war? I'd rather have Barton help me and my children than see him hanged. That money's no good just stuck in the ground.'

'She's right, Harrison. We'll split it three ways, everybody wins.' Seeing the mistrust in his captor's eyes Barton added, 'I'd be a fool to run or double-cross either of you. You draw faster than I can spit and Maggie can track a man better than an Apache.'

Harrison nodded reluctantly. 'All right. I must be crazy but I'll go along with it.'

Maggie Sloane dropped her rifle, flung her arms around his neck and hugged him tightly to her bosom. 'Oh you really are a true gentleman after all, Mister Gentleman Jack Harrison!'

'Now we're more familiar, just call me John,' he replied, smiling.

'If that's settled, will someone untie me?' asked Barton.

Harrison obliged and gave him a revolver that had belonged to one of the dead Mexicans. They also took dried beef, biscuits and water supplies from the men's saddle-bags before they turned and headed for the border. They emerged from the cool shade of the canyon into an arid landscape, but one dotted with mesquite, creosote and yucca plants. Yellow flowering acacia trees added a dash of colour to this basin region of West Texas on the edge of the Chihuahua Desert. The Sierra Madre Mountains and the Pecos River lay still further west under a shimmering blue sky. It was a long way from home and very different from his native Virginia, but Harrison had grown to love the landscape for its grandeur. Since the war he had wandered ever further to the south west, hunting outlaws throughout the region.

Yes, it was the war that had changed him, as it had changed so many. He discovered that he was handier with a gun than most men and hesitated less when his own life was threatened. He also lost his enthusiasm for good causes after witnessing the savagery they unleashed, and his taste for making distinctions of class and colour. He could never forget the well-bred gentlemen of Richmond who set fire to the city's storehouses so that the hated Yankees would not get their hands on fresh supplies. In doing so they burned half the residential district and his home and family along with it. A senseless, stupid act committed when the war was already lost. Yet it was the despised Yankees who put the flames out, of course. If only they could have saved his lovely, laughing Elizabeth and daughter Annie, only two years old when the fighting started. How they both wept the day he went off to fight in his new lieutenant's uniform and how he wept on the day of his desertion when he knelt among the charred ruins. Well, it was too late to wish he'd stayed with them and his father's law practice. Once he might have become a judge, now he was content just to catch criminals.

It was Maggie who interrupted his thoughts. 'How did a fancy fella like you finish up as a bounty hunter?'

'A man tried to rob me when I was

riding out of Virginia after the war. I shot him in self defence and took his body into the nearest town. It turned out that there was a price on his head which I collected.'

'And you just carried on doing the same thing?'

'I didn't know what else to do, I guess.' He shrugged, trying to appear nonchalant.

'I guess you just couldn't go back to your old ways, huh?'

'No old ways left to go back to in my case.' Harrison swallowed hard.

'Don't you have any family back in Virginia?'

'My father died in '64 and my mother followed a month later. My brother had been killed at the start of the war and they never got over it . . . ' He faltered for a moment before he went on. 'My wife and daughter died in the war too.'

Maggie reached across and squeezed his arm. 'I'm so sorry, John. And to think, all I've done since we met is go on about my troubles!'

Harrison smiled reassuringly. 'Oh, that's just natural. You've lost your husband and you've your children to think about. It's not easy to take care of the living while you're mourning the dead.'

'Still, I'm luckier than some and right now I know my ma will be taking good care of those boys, so . . . ' Maggie's voice trailed away as she pointed silently ahead. Barton had stopped and Harrison turned to look as they both drew in behind him.

The burnt-out remains of a stagecoach lay directly in their path, a blackened arm hanging out of the window. All around were scattered the charred remains of the other passengers and the possessions the attackers had decided not to take with them. Suitcases lay broken open, their contents spilling out. Harrison dismounted and knelt among the debris. His hand searched among broken spectacles, torn clothes and a bent umbrella until he found the item

27

he was looking for. It was a girl's doll, clad in a white silk dress. The hair was blond, the eyes cornflower blue. He was sure it was the same one he'd bought Annie the day before he rode off to fight.

Holding the doll, he smelled the burned flesh and once again he was there, at Richmond. His vision blurred by tears, he called out, 'Annie! Oh Annie, forgive me!' and collapsed sobbing to the ground.

'For God's sake, Harrison, we gotta get outa here! What if them Injuns come back?' Barton was pulling roughly at his arm and, in a split second, grief turned to rage. Harrison lashed out with his fist and the other man staggered back. Then there was a gun in his hand and the click was loud in the silence as he thumbed back the hammer. Barton did not go for his own gun, knowing he would be dead before he reached his holster.

'OK, easy Harrison, easy. Nobody wants to fight but we have to get goin' if there's Comanches on the warpath.'

Maggie was beside him now, a comforting arm around his shoulders. 'Please John, he's right. We can't stay here. There's nothing we can do for these poor folks.'

'Except bury what's left of them.' Harrison lowered his gun, breathing deeply.

Barton got back on his horse, eyes scanning the horizon. 'Ain't no time for that,' he muttered impatiently.

'I'm not a religious man, not any more. But everyone deserves a decent burial, even a weasel like you, Barton.'

'Well, I don't plan on gettin' buried any time soon. If *you* do then just stick around here long enough.'

Harrison shook his head. 'Those Comanches will be long gone, assuming it was them. It could have been outlaws or bandits, hard to tell. There's good and bad in all kinds of men. I learned that much during the war. That's what makes sense to me, Clay. We don't know where the people who did this went but there's no reason to think they'll be coming back.'

'Well, all right, but I ain't doin' no diggin,' said Barton defiantly.

Harrison did most of the work with some help from Maggie, while Barton sat sullenly on his mount. When it was over he said a brief prayer to the god he hoped was there somewhere, out of a sense of propriety at least. Then they were on their way again, but the journey continued in silence for some time. They passed over a creek where they watered the horses and refreshed themselves before moving up to higher ground as they crossed a low lying range. As evening fell Barton pointed to a cave up ahead. 'We could make camp there, then head for Jacob's Well tomorrow,' he suggested.

'Isn't that a mission of some sort? Strange place for you to be stopping,' remarked Harrison.

'Yeah, but there's a good tradin' post there, where we can get supplies and rest up. The money's buried two days' ride further on from it.'

Harrison was distracted by a sudden flashing light against the sunset. He turned and saw that Maggie was preening herself in front of a small hand held mirror, the light reflecting against the rocks on a steep canyon to the east of them. 'Hey, stop that foolishness!' he cried as he seized her wrist. 'After what we've seen today the last thing we should do is risk drawing attention to ourselves. We don't know who might be over there. Do you want us to be spotted?'

She snapped the compact mirror shut immediately. 'You're right, I'm sorry. It's hard for a woman to stop trying to look her best.'

'Well, them Comanches might appreciate it. Fancy bein' a squaw?' jeered Barton.

'Better than the saloon-bar whores you're used to I expect,' she replied tartly.

'Gimme a saloon-bar whore any day. They don't talk back to a fella, I'll say that for 'em,' chuckled Barton.

Nothing further was said then as they headed wearily for the cave. Harrison gathered some sagebrush for a fire and they settled down to a meal of dried beef, beans, biscuits and coffee before laying out their bedrolls to sleep. Harrison was exhausted and for once his sleep was undisturbed by nightmares from the past.

The sun was barely up before he felt someone shaking him awake. His eyes blinked open and saw Maggie's face looming above his own, her features a mask of anxiety. 'For God's sake, John, wake up!' she hissed urgently.

'What is it?' Harrison sat up, rubbing his face.

'That goddamn snake Barton's gone. He took the horses, all our food and water. What are we going to do?'

Harrison was on his feet in a moment. He ran to the mouth of the cave and peered out but saw nothing in the distance. He shook his head. 'Barton's long gone, I'm afraid. Must have left hours ago.'

'He knows we can't catch up with him on foot and how long can we last out here with no supplies?' Maggie shook her head from side to side, despair etched on her face.

'Wait a minute. Didn't he say there's a mission and trading post not far from here, Jacob's Well?'

She snorted. 'Not far if you've a horse and you're not dying of thirst!'

Harrison shrugged. 'Look, it's our only chance. Besides, there are wild plants we can eat and get some moisture from. If we're lucky we might just make it, especially if we pass a creek on the way where we can get a drink.'

Maggie stood up. 'It's not too hot out there yet. I guess the further we get before noon the better.'

Harrison nodded. 'All right, we're wasting time here. Let's go.'

His gunbelt was still beside him and he buckled it on. Barton had been smart enough not to risk disturbing him by taking that as well, and at least it meant they could defend themselves if they had to. He strode ahead with more confidence than he felt as Maggie followed him out of the cave. The hills on either side provided some shelter from the sun and they made good progress for a couple of hours as they descended to the basin below. Once out in the open plain, however, they began to feel the heat. By midday Harrison was wondering how much longer he could go on. His mouth felt like sawdust, his string tie, coat and waistcoat had been cast aside and his shirt clung to his back. Maggie stumbled along beside him, her breath coming in short gasps. The vegetation in this particular area was quite sparse and they had passed nothing that could be of any use to them.

'It's no good, I've got to rest,' whispered Maggie. She slumped on to a large rock.

'All right, just for a minute, but then we've got to keep moving.'

'Oh, what's the use? We'll die out here anyway.'

Harrison was too weary himself to reply and he sat down beside her. At that moment he heard a trundling sound in the distance. Shading his eyes with his hand he looked around and saw a speck which gradually emerged as a wagon coming towards them from the east. Shouting hoarsely, he jumped up and waved his arms. Maggie looked up then, and drew out her compact mirror, which she held up until it flashed against the sun.

'Do you think he's seen us?' she asked excitedly.

'Well, he's still coming this way so he will soon enough, anyhow.'

The wagon which approached them was brightly painted with an advertisement for *Dr Gabriel's Elixir of Life Which Cures Every Ill Known to Man*. It was hung with tassels, tiny bells and velvet curtains. The driver had a waxed moustache and a pointed black beard below a pair of steel rimmed spectacles perched on the end of his nose. His black top hat and matching coat were presumably intended to give the impression, undoubtedly false, that here was a man endowed with superior knowledge, not a quack peddling fake remedies.

'Can you help us?' asked Harrison. 'Our horses and all our provisions were stolen but I've some money in my pocket and can pay you for your trouble.'

The driver spread his arms expansively. 'Can I help you? Of course, sir and you too, dear madam. Allow me to introduce myself.' Sweeping off his hat with a flourish he performed a low bow as he continued, 'I am Doctor Leo Gabriel, purveyor of ancient wisdom lost since the time of the Egyptians, potions that can guarantee long life, but also furs, trade goods and good old-fashioned whiskey.'

'We just want some food, water and a ride to Jacob's Well,' said Maggie wearily.

Gabriel smiled and threw them a canteen, from which they each drank greedily. 'By all means climb aboard my chariot, dear friends. You'll find cool shade and food in the back, but I must use my trade in the service of the noble savage before we reach your destination.'

'You trade with the Comanches?' Harrison's eyes narrowed. 'We saw the remains of a stagecoach yesterday and what was left of its passengers. Was that their handiwork?'

Gabriel shook his head sadly. 'I fear it was, but don't judge me.' He held up a white gloved hand. 'By trading with them I remain safe and can also tell what their mood is, whether for peace or war. The soldiers at Fort Concho have had reason to be glad of that information.'

'Will it be safe for us too?'

'Have no fear. To the Comanches you too will be persons protected by the Great Spirit.'

Harrison shrugged. They seemed to have no choice other than to trust this huckster. Even with food and water, he was not sure that they could make it alive to Jacob's Well on foot. They climbed into the back of the wagon and made themselves comfortable, chewing on some dried fruit and biscuits as they trundled on their way.

An hour passed before the smell of campfires drifted towards them on the breeze as they approached the temporary settlement the Comanches had established. They were a nomadic people, unlike the Apaches who lived in settled communities, and this was presumably a convenient spot from which to launch raids on small towns, wagon trains and isolated ranches. Harrison had some sympathy for their plight, as the buffalo herds they relied upon were decimated by white hunters, the lands they had been used to roam freely were turned into cattle ranches and they themselves were pushed on to small reservations. This band, in common with other Comanche groups, had obviously decided to fight back.

As he alighted from the wagon, Harrison saw that the camp was a hive of activity. There were warriors mending arrows, loading rifles and sharpening spears, while others led their horses out from the area where they were corralled. Many of them wore buckskin shirts and all had long, braided hair. Women scurried in and out of the hundred or so tepees scattered about, fetching provisions.

Maggie was walking by his side, with Gabriel just in front. The 'doctor' was gesturing animatedly and speaking in a mixture of the Comanche language and his own. The Comanche did not seem pleased by their presence, however. One of their number approached and, pointing at Harrison and Maggie, demanded of Gabriel, 'Why you bring them here?'

'They are friends, Swift Eagle; they help me bring you many fine things. Come, come and see.' Gabriel gestured towards the wagon and a crowd gathered as he opened it up to reveal the bottles of whiskey, blankets, buffalo hides and other goods inside.

Swift Eagle nodded curtly. 'Your people are our enemies but you we have not harmed. Soon great trouble shall come to the whites who steal from us.

So now we take from you and send you back to your people with this warning.' Then, as the crowd moved forward to empty the wagon of its goods, a dishevelled captive, stripped to the waist and covered in cuts, bruises and burns was pushed towards them. Harrison's mouth set firmly in a grimace. The man was Clay Barton.

3

Barton appeared barely conscious as he stumbled forward before falling against Gabriel, who quickly moved to steady him.

'You've got a poor exchange there, I'm afraid. That's the man who robbed us.' Harrison fingered the handle of his gun, sorely tempted to shoot.

'Hmm. Revenge is all very well but a man who commits one crime is sometimes wanted for another. Are you sure he's of no value?'

'He killed a guard escaping from prison. In Tucson his corpse is worth a thousand dollars. Alive he's worth at least a hundred times that amount.' Harrison exchanged glances with Maggie who nodded her approval. She probably felt sorry for Gabriel just as much as he did. The man had saved their lives and now he had lost all his goods. Being honest with him and sharing the loot, assuming they ever found it, seemed like the right thing to do.

Gabriel bundled Barton into the back of the wagon. 'Very well, friend, you can explain on the way, but for now I'd recommend a swift departure.'

Harrison heaved a sigh of relief as they left the camp and the hostile stares of the Comanches. 'Swift Eagle seemed to be the man in charge back there.'

Gabriel nodded. 'He's one of their toughest warriors. My guess is they've chosen him as a war chief and they're planning to launch an attack soon, probably against Jacob's Well.'

'I guess travellers in these parts really depend on that trading post. I hope it doesn't get destroyed.'

'It's difficult to say. If Jacob's Well could be defended and the attack driven off the Comanches might think again, provided their losses are heavy enough. That could be the end of it. Otherwise, they'll move on to other towns, maybe even attack Fort Concho.

That's the headquarters of the Tenth Cavalry.'

'Aren't they the ones the Comanche call Buffalo Soldiers?'

Gabriel chuckled. 'Great soldiers; some of them used to be slaves.'

'I fought against Negro regiments during the war. They were incredibly brave, changed my opinion about a lot of things,' Harrison told him.

'Well, a troop of them was sent over to Jacob's Well yesterday, so there's a good chance it can be defended. Anyway, it's the safest place to be until all this is over. I don't rate our chances of survival in open country with those Comanches on the warpath.' Gabriel laughed as Harrison looked around nervously.

'I wouldn't worry just yet. There was enough whiskey on this wagon to keep them occupied, at least until tomorrow.' Changing the subject, he asked, 'So what about this money your friend has?'

Harrison snorted. 'He's no friend of

anyone's, I can assure you of that.' He proceeded to tell the story of Barton's capture, subsequent treachery over the hidden money, and Maggie's involvement. 'It's probably best if we keep him tied up until he's done what he promised and led us to the money,' he concluded.

Gabriel glanced into the back of the wagon where Maggie was reluctantly tending Barton's wounds. 'He still looks very weak, won't be trying to go anywhere for a while.' He fished inside his coat pocket and pulled out a bottle of dark liquid. 'Besides, this should keep him quiet for a few days.'

'What is it?'

'Laudanum. People can get too fond of it and end up seeing things that aren't there, but if he isn't used to it he'll just sleep.'

Despite his antipathy towards Barton, Harrison was troubled by the idea of keeping him drugged but told himself the man was getting off lightly after all he had done. He looked back towards Maggie and smiled at the sight of her nursing a man she had every right to wish dead. Somehow, he felt certain that for all her feistiness, hers was a heart that did not harbour the desire for revenge. He did not know why, but he found that thought comforting.

'We're here,' said Gabriel as a settlement of adobe and wooden buildings, surrounded by a low wall, came into view. As they drove through Harrison noticed that there was a general store, hotel, saloon bar, livery stables and a church with what appeared to be a small school attached to it.

'I think I'll take a look around,' he said, jumping down as the wagon slowed to a halt at the stables. He went first to the general store, conscious of his soiled shirt and dishevelled appearance. Harrison always wore clothes which most men, even if they possessed such items, would consider their 'Sunday best' and the storekeeper was surprised when he selected the only suit in stock, a white shirt and a string tie. He added spare clothing, a razor and soap to the pile before using the pump in the back yard to wash and shave. Once dressed in his new clothes he returned to the street and approached Gabriel, who was talking to an army officer, a tall slender man with an erect bearing.

'This is Lieutenant Schmidt; he's in command here.'

'Good afternoon, Lieutenant, I'm John Harrison.'

The officer nodded curtly. 'Gabriel here was telling me about your encounter with the Indians. How many of them were there, do you think?' He spoke in a clipped tone with a pronounced German accent.

'It was difficult to tell; at least a hundred, I'd say.'

Schmidt shook his head impatiently. 'I've less than fifty of this rabble to fight them with,' he said, gesturing towards the black-skinned soldiers who were helping to reinforce the walls.

'I think you'll find they acquit themselves well in battle, Lieutenant,' remarked Harrison stiffly.

'We'll find out soon enough. I hope for all our sakes that you're right.' Schmidt turned away to bark orders at his men while Harrison and Gabriel headed for the stables, where Maggie was continuing to tend Barton in the wagon.

'How is he?' asked Gabriel, peering anxiously at the bound, huddled figure.

'He's sleeping a lot. What was that stuff you gave him earlier?' she enquired.

Harrison cut in. 'Don't worry, it won't do him any harm, but he won't be getting up to any of his tricks.' Then he added, 'If we're not careful, he'll take the wagon and be off again.'

Maggie sighed. 'I know that well enough, but he's still human, whatever he may have done. We couldn't have left him to be tortured to death anyway, never mind the money.'

Harrison felt bound to agree. He was glad there were people like Maggie to remind him of how much goodness there was in the world, something he forgot at times. 'I'll be in the saloon if anyone needs me,' he said as he left.

After a decent meal, followed by a haze of whiskey, he collapsed into a fitful sleep at the hotel, punctuated by the dreams which had haunted his nights for the past ten years.

Harrison bathed as the sun rose, then went downstairs for breakfast. 'It seems very quiet here,' he said as the maid poured him some coffee.

The girl looked around nervously. 'They say the Comanches are comin'. A lot of folks just upped and left. I'm not sure if I should stay here myself.'

'You'll be safer here than in the open country. We can build barricades, there are soldiers to protect us and every man who's got a gun will fight.'

'I hope you're right, mister. I've never been so scared.'

'There's no shame in being afraid, but at least you're not alone here,' Harrison told her.

Outside the atmosphere was tense. The walls were lined with soldiers, each armed with a Winchester '73 repeating rifle. Harrison approached Schmidt, who was peering through a telescope for signs of the enemy approaching.

'Excuse me, Lieutenant.'

'Yes, what is it?' asked Schmidt without turning around.

'I was wondering if I might have a rifle.'

The telescope was snapped shut as the officer turned to face him. 'Don't you have one of your own?'

'I had one of those revolving rifles but it was stolen when I was on the way here, along with my horse and other things.'

Schmidt nodded slowly. 'Ah yes, your friend Gabriel told me yesterday. Very well. I hope you're a good shot, Harrison.' He turned to a burly black sergeant standing near him. 'Johnson, get this man a rifle and ammunition.' The man saluted smartly and went off at the double, returning moments later with a Winchester and some bullets.

Harrison loaded hurriedly and took

his place at a gap in the wall alongside another civilian. It was the storekeeper, a sombre-looking man in owlish spectacles. The two exchanged silent nods of greeting as they settled down to take aim.

At that moment a cloud of dust appeared in the distance, accompanied by a high-pitched war cry. The bugle sounded and Schmidt ordered them to take aim. The cloud moved closer and soon both men and horses were clearly visible. As they came within range the order was made and a volley of gunfire erupted from the walls. Harrison aimed at a warrior who rode high in the saddle of a white horse, brandishing a lance. He squeezed the trigger and saw him fall back as if flung to the ground by an invisible giant. Others were also falling as many of the shots hit home.

As the Comanches advanced he noticed that some of them wore trophies from previous battles. One was clad in a colonel's jacket and a stovepipe hat. Harrison fired again and watched with grim satisfaction as the bullet reached its target. Just then an arrow whizzed past his ear. The Comanches were excellent horsemen and were able to lean over the flanks of their mounts to protect themselves as they fired their weapons, although few of them had rifles. Soon the troops were coming under attack from well aimed arrows and lances. Soldiers cried out as they were hit and fell back from the wall. Stretcher bearers hurriedly took them to the church, which had been turned into a makeshift hospital.

The bugle sounded again and Schmidt led a cavalry charge of the troops he had been keeping in reserve to engage the enemy at close quarters. Dust was thrown up as a mêlée of thrusting, stabbing and shooting ensued. The Comanches fell back at first but then attacked with renewed force. The men at the wall retreated as they continued to fire at the warriors who were breaking through in an effort to surround them. Harrison heard a sharp cry above the gunfire and turned to see the store-keeper fall sideways, an arrow protruding from between his shoulder blades. He swung around sharply and fired at the war-painted warrior responsible, who was now aiming at him. The man's hands flew up to his face as he tumbled from his horse.

There were Comanches riding along the dusty street, clubbing soldiers with tomahawks, firing revolvers and shooting arrows all around them. The men of the Tenth Cavalry fought back, turning from the wall to fight the enemy hand to hand. Harrison put his rifle aside and whipped both guns from their holsters. Crossing the street, he fired into the throng, dodging the rearing hoofs as more Comanches fell dying from their horses.

Suddenly Sergeant Johnson was at his side, yelling above the noise of battle. 'Can you cover me while I get across to the store? I got an idea!' Harrison nodded and fired at any warrior who had Johnson in his range as the cavalryman sprinted across to his destination. Moments later he emerged with a box of firecrackers, one of which he had already lit and flung under the hoofs of a warrior's horse. The creature bucked and reared as its owner struggled to stay on its back, making him an easy target for Harrison. Crouching in a doorway, Johnson lit more of the firecrackers and soon more than a dozen terrified horses were bolting and throwing their owners to the ground. Those still alive were quickly shot or bayoneted.

The Comanches started to fall back now, but a new threat emerged as some agile warriors climbed on to the rooftops. From there they fired at the soldiers below with rifles they had seized from the dead, while others set buildings alight. Harrison rounded up a few of the younger men and they clambered up after the Indians from a backyard behind the stables.

Advancing up a sloping roof, they emerged behind a Comanche who heard their approach and swung round with his Winchester just as Harrison fired. He fell back, clutching his chest before tumbling into a water trough below with a loud splash. Waving his gun, Harrison urged the men to spread out as they leaped on to neighbouring buildings. He landed on the lower roof of the church and looked up to see a Comanche in a leather waistcoat shooting from the bell tower. He rolled sideways as the man fired at him, but his returning shot hit the rifle so that it tumbled uselessly from the shooter's hands. The Comanche leaned out to throw a knife and Harrison's second shot hit him squarely between the eyes.

He turned back to view the chaotic scene below. There were men engaged in vicious combat, the street was littered with bloodstained corpses and several buildings were now ablaze. Beyond the walls, the cavalry continued to hold off the remaining Comanches who had not managed to break through, but it was far from over yet. Harrison's eyes narrowed as he spotted a familiar figure, one of the tallest among the Comanches, who shouted and waved as he tried to rally his followers. It was Swift Eagle, riding a magnificent black stallion. Harrison leaped down just as the war chief galloped below and the two men hit the ground in a grappling heap. Swift Eagle rolled beneath him, flung him to one side and came at him with a knife as Harrison jumped to his feet. He managed to seize the Comanche's wrist in time to deflect the blow, then lashed out with his boot to send his opponent sprawling in the dirt. Swift Eagle sprang up like a tiger, but Harrison's gun was in his hand. He fired just as another warrior came between them on horseback before tumbling to the ground. Then the Comanche was gone.

Harrison looked around and spied his quarry sprinting towards the stables. His heart thudded against his chest as he thought of Maggie minding the wagon and the team of horses. He ran after Swift Eagle and went inside. Then he froze for a moment. There was only silence and the smell of hay, no sign of Maggie, the wagon or the Comanche. Suddenly, there was a war cry and a stamping of hoofs as Swift Eagle emerged from the shadows on a chestnut mare. Harrison was taken by surprise and fired blindly, wounding the animal in the flank. It reared in pain as the rider tumbled backwards on to the ground, where he lay stunned. Harrison quickly placed his foot on Swift Eagle's chest as the horse bolted for the door. 'Going somewhere?' he enquired casually as he pointed his gun at him.

At that moment Johnson entered the stable with two of his men following close behind. The Comanche was quickly hauled to his feet, bound and hustled away, eyes blazing.

'I'm glad you had the sense not to shoot,' Johnson told him. 'We can hold him as a hostage over at Fort Concho, get his people to make peace that way.'

The two men stepped outside to find that the noise of battle had died down and the remaining Comanches were in retreat. However, the church was now ablaze and buckets of water were being passed along a line of soldiers and civilians to try to put out the flames. The dead were covered with blankets and taken away for burial by stretcher bearers. It was a horrific scene but Harrison had witnessed far worse in the past.

'I was looking for the people I was with but I can't see any sign of them,' he said.

'Didn't they tell you they was leavin'? The sergeant appeared puzzled and Harrison was now even more concerned.

'Did you see them go?'

'Yeah, this mornin' before all hell broke loose. As I remember it the lady was sittin' up front with Doctor Gabriel, as he calls hisself. She didn't look none too pleased, I can tell you that much, and there was a mean-lookin' fella with a scar on his face between 'em. Looked like they were headed towards the border.'

Harrison nodded grimly. Now it all made sense. Gabriel thought that while the Comanches were busy attacking Jacob's Well he would not be at risk out in the open and had decided to double-cross him for a bigger share of the money, or perhaps all of it. Surely Maggie would not agree to such a plan? She must have been taken along by force, presumably to prevent her from warning him.

'Where's Lieutenant Schmidt?' he demanded.

Johnson pointed towards the wall. 'He's just back from drivin' off them Comanches.'

'I've got to talk to him. Would you mind coming along?'

'Sure, if it'll help.'

Schmidt was dismounting as they approached. 'I've just been informed that you captured the leader of those savages. Well done, Harrison.'

'Sergeant Johnson also helped, Lieutenant. In fact, it was his quick thinking with the firecrackers that really saved the day.'

Schmidt grunted in response. He was not an officer given to praising his men.

'Well, what can I do for you?'

'The lady I arrived with has been kidnapped by Gabriel. I think she's in great danger.'

Schmidt smiled mirthlessly. 'I was not aware that you had such a taste for melodrama, Harrison or that you were sentimental about women. Has it not occurred to you that she may have gone willingly? Go after her if you must, but I wouldn't recommend it.'

Harrison fought down his rising anger. 'No, Lieutenant, I'm sure that what you say is untrue. Mrs Sloane is a grieving widow and would not have gone off with a man she hardly knows, certainly not without talking to me first.'

'It may be as you say,' acknowledged Schmidt grudgingly, 'but it's not my affair. I can't send my men chasing through the desert after ladies in distress.'

Harrison drew in a deep breath and let it out. He had made up his mind. 'Can you send them after a hundred thousand dollars stolen from an army payroll and the murdering thief who knows where it's hidden?'

He had Schmidt's full attention now. 'What are you talking about?'

Harrison briefly told him about Barton, Maggie, the stolen money and how Gabriel had become involved.

Schmidt was breathing heavily now. Grabbing Harrison's lapel, he leaned forward and demanded, 'This Barton, does he have a scar on his face?'

'Yes. What of it?'

'I gave him that scar.' Schmidt released his grip before continuing. 'Five years ago I was a captain escorting a payroll wagon when we were attacked. We killed most of them but one escaped with a strongbox full of money. I cut him with my sword before he got away. I heard later that he'd been caught, but the money was never found. There weren't enough men on the job and someone had to take the blame.'

'That someone being you, I suppose?'

'That's right, Harrison. I had to face a court martial and was demoted before being transferred. Now I must be the

60

oldest lieutenant in the army!'

'Well, now's your chance to get even.'

'I intend to. Look, we'll rescue your lady friend for you and give you a thousand dollars from the strongbox, but Barton's mine, understood?'

Harrison nodded. 'You can try taking him prisoner if you want to. He's brought me nothing but trouble.'

'This time he won't escape, I promise you that.'

Harrison shivered. He had a feeling that Schmidt was a man who would administer his own justice.

4

The battle-weary Schmidt was suddenly decisive and full of energy. 'Johnson, you're coming with us. I'll tell Sergeant Collins to take command while I'm gone. Get Wilcox and Coley as well.' The sergeant saluted smartly and was gone.

'Barton said the money is buried about two days' ride from here, on the way to the Mexican border,' Harrison told him.

Schmidt rubbed his hand over his jaw thoughtfully. 'Hmm. There's an abandoned silver mine in that area. Could that be the place?'

Harrison shrugged. 'It's probably the best place to look if we can't pick up their trail, but we need to get going in any case. They've had a few hours' start.'

Schmidt was confident. 'We'll leave as soon as the supplies are ready and take the best horses. If we don't stop until after dark and rise early we'll catch them up.'

'It will probably take some time to dig up the money. It might be best to stay just out of sight and then surprise Gabriel and Barton while they're in the act.'

'Perhaps, but just remember one thing, Harrison. This is a military operation and I'm in charge. That means I'll be giving the orders.' The hint of menace in Schmidt's tone made Harrison feel uneasy.

'I stopped following orders a long time ago, but I'll try not to get in your way. I am a civilian, after all.'

Schmidt nodded reluctantly. 'All right, just as long as you make yourself useful.'

They were ready to leave within the hour, Schmidt taking the lead. Harrison disliked the man, an arrogant martinet who despised the men under his command, but he was impressed by the energy and drive he showed so soon after fighting a battle. As they passed the church, he saw that the flames had been put out, but the building was little more than a blackened shell.

The wounded had been moved outside under a makeshift canopy and were being tended by the survivors. Harrison felt torn between an urge to help them and his concern for Maggie but he focused his gaze on the horizon and rode straight ahead.

The heat and dust of the journey soon drove the images of suffering from his mind. Schmidt continued in the lead, in front while Johnson rode beside Harrison. Wilcox and Coley brought up the rear. Wilcox was short, squat and the lighter-skinned of the two, while Coley, who wore a corporal's stripes, had a tall, elongated figure. His ebony features appeared carefully chiselled, with high cheekbones and an aquiline nose, giving him a regal bearing.

Johnson informed him of the men's backgrounds. 'Wilcox, back there, was born on a plantation in Louisiana. He ran away to join the army when the war broke out. Now, Coley, he's from New

Jersey, never been no slave.' He turned his head and called back to their companions. 'Am I right fellas?'

Coley answered for both of them. 'That's right, Sergeant. Wilcox here just got sick o' pickin' other men's cotton. Me, I'll be as free as I want when I'm a general.'

'What about you, Sergeant? Where are you from?' Harrison asked.

'New Orleans. My daddy was a blacksmith who saved enough to buy his own freedom. He managed to teach me the trade but I didn't really take to it much, just wanted a life of adventure, I guess.'

'Is this adventurous enough for you?'

Johnson frowned then. 'I hope it don't get too adventurous, Mr Harrison. We could run into a heap o' trouble before we even reach this mine. We may have licked them Comanches but there could still be some out here might attack us, not to mention the bandits sellin' 'em guns and robbin' folks.'

'We'd better keep alert then.'

At that moment Schmidt raised his hand to halt them. He turned in the saddle, then pointed ahead. 'Do those look like fresh wagon tracks to you?'

Harrison dismounted to examine them more closely. 'Yes, they do. Could they be theirs? They'd move faster without the wagon, though.'

'Gabriel probably thought the Comanches would keep us busy for a couple of days. Besides, you can't move too quickly in this heat.' Schmidt mopped his brow with a large white handkerchief before drinking some water from a canteen.

'Are we to follow those tracks then, sir?' asked Johnson.

'Yes. They lead in the direction of the mine anyway.'

They were about a mile further on when they saw a man lying spread-eagled on the ground just to the right of them. He was stripped to the waist with his hands and feet bound to stakes driven into the ground. A group of vultures approached his prone figure and he made groans and weak movements to frighten them away. He had obviously been there for a while as the vultures were no longer keeping their distance. One had perched on his knee, refusing to be dislodged and was about to sink its beak into his flesh as Harrison clapped his hands and shouted, causing the creature to fly a short distance away. Johnson had dismounted by this time and hurried over to the man, scattering the other birds. Raising his head he carefully dribbled water between his parched lips, speaking soothingly to him as he did so. The others gathered around as Johnson drew a knife to cut the captive's bonds.

'Johnson, what are you doing?' asked Schmidt with undisguised annoyance.

'The man needs help, sir.' The sergeant's tone was calm but puzzled. 'He says bandits did this to him.'

'For God's sake, man, can't you see he's almost dead?'

'Almost but not quite,' added Harrison. 'That's an important distinction.'

'Stay out of this!' Schmidt appeared really angry now as he too dismounted and strode up behind Johnson. 'Look, we can't take him with us. He'll slow us down and probably die on the way.'

Johnson stood up and turned to face the lieutenant. 'I'll put him on my horse, sir. I'll take good care of him and . . . '

'Your job is to follow orders, not play nursemaid, damn you! Stand to attention when you address me!'

Johnson stood upright, saluted smartly and then added softly, 'We can't just leave him here to die, sir.'

Schmidt appeared to relax suddenly and even smiled at the sergeant. 'You're right, we have to relieve his suffering.'

The lieutenant drew his officer's sword and approached the prisoner. He raised the weapon slightly but then, instead of cutting him free, thrust it deep into his heart. The bound man writhed briefly before he stiffened and lay still. In the shocked silence that followed Schmidt turned back to his sergeant and bellowed, 'Now get your black hide back on that horse before I use it on you!'

Johnson showed no fear but his eyes were filled with a deep hatred as he stared back at the officer. He stood still, his fists clenched at his sides.

'I gave you an order!' shrieked Schmidt, his face crimson with rage. He moved a step closer as he brandished his bloodstained sword in front of the sergeant's face.

'That's enough, Schmidt!' said Harrison sharply. 'No one gives a damn about your orders any more.' He drew his gun and thumbed back the hammer as the officer turned towards him.

'Drop it or I'll blow your head off.' Schmidt froze as he stared at the revolver. 'I'm not one of your troops and if a man points a weapon at me I've got the right to defend myself.' Harrison spoke quietly but there was no mistaking the edge in his tone. Schmidt knew he was not bluffing. Slowly, he lowered the sword and Harrison put his gun away.

Wilcox and Coley dismounted to help Johnson and Harrison bury the dead man. This time Schmidt said nothing but sat waiting on his horse until they had finished. Then, wordlessly, he spurred his mount to ride on in front as an uneasy silence descended on the group.

It grew cooler at sunset as they approached a rocky area divided by a narrow creek. The horses drank their fill and rested as the men refilled their canteens. Coley pointed to some wagon tracks just ahead of them. Dropping to his haunches he examined them closely.

'It looks like we're not far behind,' he remarked thoughtfully.

'There must be a canyon up ahead. It could be a good place to make camp if we get there by nightfall,' said Johnson, pointing to some higher ground in the distance.

'It is a canyon,' said Schmidt as he peered through his telescope. It was the first time he had spoken since his actions earlier that day and he did not look at his companions as he did so, nor did they look at him. He snapped the instrument shut and rode on ahead. The others fell in behind. An orange globe dropped behind the peaks as they reached their destination. A cave provided shelter and Harrison took the first watch once they had finished the dried beef, beans and coffee prepared by Wilcox. Johnson relieved him a couple of hours later.

Despite the horrors of the day, he enjoyed a deep and dreamless sleep. The others were all deep in slumber as he roused himself, apart from Schmidt who was sitting up against a boulder with his shoulders wrapped by a blanket and a rifle across his knees. It seemed that he had taken the last watch of the night. Harrison noticed the pool of blood between the officer's knees as he stepped past him.

He put a hand on Schmidt's shoulder and shook him gently. The dead man's head rolled back and Harrison found himself gazing into a pair of sightless eyes. Lieutenant Schmidt's throat had been slit from ear to ear.

Harrison gasped as he stepped backwards, knocking the empty coffee pot over on to the tin plates. Johnson woke with a start and sat upright, asking what was wrong.

'See for yourself, assuming you don't know already,' replied Harrison, gesturing towards the corpse.

Johnson looked down at the body of his commanding officer and shook his head. 'Now wait a minute, mister. I won't pretend to be sorry but I didn't do this, wouldn't kill a man like that in cold blood no matter what he'd done.'

Wilcox and Coley were both awake now. 'I don't suppose either of you two know anything about this?' Harrison asked them.

Wilcox shook his head in horrified puzzlement. Coley did not speak but was busy buckling on his gunbelt.

'Corporal, you've been asked a question,' Johnson reminded him.

'He had it comin', y'all know that,' muttered Coley with a shrug of indifference.

72

Johnson shook his head vigorously. 'He sure did but that don't make it right. You crossed a line, boy.'

Coley nodded. 'Yeah, maybe I did. Maybe I've wanted to cross that line a long time. Maybe I'm tired of all the dirt that gets kicked in my face on account of my skin, the dirt that gets kicked in all our faces.'

Johnson nodded. 'I'm tired of it too, man, but damn it, you should be better than this.'

Harrison spoke next. 'The question is, what happens now? I don't approve of what Coley's done but I'm not about to put a rope around his neck for it.'

'I guess we'll have to bury Schmidt out here and figure out some story to explain it before we get back,' said Johnson reluctantly.

Wilcox and Coley exchanged looks. 'There's at least a hundred thousand dollars buried some place in that old mine,' Coley reminded the sergeant. 'We could be over the border with it before anyone figures we're not comin' back.'

'So we're deserters now, are we?' Johnson shook his head in bewilderment. 'I've given fifteen years to the army, seen plenty of good men die and now you want me to just run away. Is that it?'

'What have you got to show for all those years?' Wilcox asked him. 'You'll be a sergeant 'til you get killed or retire. How many officers do you see who ain't white?'

'Yeah, and there'll always be another Schmidt to push you around,' added Coley.

Johnson sat down on a rock as he thought. 'Guess I can't stop you if that's what you figure on doin', but it don't seem right. I'll have to go back.'

Coley snorted. 'They won't be givin' you a medal for turnin' up without your men, the money or your commandin' officer.'

Johnson nodded. 'Yeah, they'll want someone to blame, I guess. Seems like I got no choice.' He turned to face Harrison. 'What do you think?'

'All I want is to see my friend rescued and to collect that thousand-dollar reward for Barton's hide. What you three men choose to do after that is up to you.'

'Well, that settles it. We'd best get goin'.' Johnson stood up decisively and they began to pack up.

Wilcox clapped the sergeant on the shoulder. 'Cheer up. Think of all them *señoritas* down in Mexico to spend some o' that money on. You'll be able to buy whatever you want.'

'It sounds like paradise, my friend.' They all turned, reaching for their weapons to see a tall, elegantly dressed figure standing in the opening of the cave.

'This ain't your business, mister, you'd best take a walk,' said Coley menacingly.

'I have two dozen men outside who say it is,' replied the stranger. As he stepped further towards them Harrison was able to study the man more closely. The Spanish style light-grey suit and ruffled shirt suggested that he was a man of some means. A mane of silver hair crowned his leonine head above a matching, neatly trimmed beard. His dark, almost black eyes were set in smooth, olive skin. Harrison judged him to be in his early fifties but in good shape with a lithe, athletic figure.

'Allow me to introduce myself, gentlemen. I am Don Pedro Felipe Gonzalez-Ortega. I have, as I said, two dozen men outside who are most anxious to make your acquaintance, so if you will be kind enough to follow me . . . '

'What do you want, Ortega?' asked Harrison.

The Mexican smiled as he took a puff from the cigar he held between two of his be-ringed fingers. 'Your conversation this morning has been most enlightening, señores. I heard every word, believe me, so what I want should be quite obvious to you.'

'Forget it. Now get outta here before I blow your Spanish ass back to Mexico.' Johnson pointed a rifle at the man's chest. At such close range, it would be impossible for him to miss.

'That would be a brave but foolhardy gesture, my friend. Do you think my men would hesitate to avenge my death? They would not and all of you would die.' Ortega's tone remained light, conversational and almost mocking, but there was an edge to it. Harrison sensed that he was used to being obeyed and not given to issuing idle threats. Reaching behind him, he placed a hand on the barrel of Johnson's weapon and gently urged him to lower it.

Ortega nodded his approval. 'I see you are a prudent man, Señor . . . Harrison, is it not? We have been following and observing you all since yesterday, beginning with that unfortunate incident after you found one of my men — '

'I presume you mean the poor wretch we found tied up?'

'Do not pity him; an army spy.' Ortega spat contemptuously. 'Before the war with Texas, my family owned lands, herds of cattle and a beautiful hacienda. Afterwards, Texas was part of the union and we were left with nothing. Now I am called a bandit, thief and outlaw by the very people who stole my inheritance, and spies are sent to betray me. Come, there has been enough talking, we must go.'

The four men looked at each other, then reluctantly followed Ortega out of the cave.

5

Ortega was not bluffing. Outside, in the glaring sunshine, two dozen mounted bandits awaited them. Harrison and his companions were made to surrender their weapons before saddling up to follow their captors along a steep path which led higher up into the canyon. Before long they reached a network of caves above a stream which had clearly been turned into a settlement of some sort. Once they had dismounted, Ortega gestured for Harrison to follow him as he ducked into the entrance to one of the caves. Oil lamps had been fastened to the walls, which had been whitewashed, and there were rushes on the floor. He followed the Mexican along a winding, narrow passageway until it broadened out into a much bigger central cave. This had actually been furnished with a desk, behind which was a high backed leather chair in which Ortega sat himself down. He gestured to a couple of smaller chairs in front of it and Harrison sat down too. Looking around he noticed that there were rugs on the floor, a mirror, wash-stand and even a divan bed.

'It is not bad eh, *señor*? These are my quarters when I am not over the border in Mexico. I have a house there but soon there will be enough for a proper ranch and a grand house, just like the old days, no?'

'I wouldn't be so certain of that, Ortega. The people we're following may get to that money ahead of us.'

'I think not. You see, I sent some of my men on ahead to that mine yesterday. They are well armed and superb horsemen and may give this Señor Gabriel a surprise.'

'How do you know that name?' asked Harrison in puzzlement.

'I told you, *señor*, you have been under observation for some time. Your conversations with the sergeant were overheard, as was the mention of a mine, although until today I did not realize its true significance. I knew from the reports I had received that you were following people there and suspected that you were in pursuit of something valuable.'

Harrison nodded. 'Pursuit is the right word. Only one man knows exactly whereabouts in that mine the money is hidden and he's with Gabriel.'

Ortega sat back in his chair as he lit a fresh cigar. He offered the box to Harrison who ignored the gesture, then shrugged and opened a drawer in his desk to pull out a crumpled, blood-stained sheet of paper which he placed on top of the pile of papers between them. It was a wanted poster for Clay Barton.

Harrison was incredulous. 'Where did you get this?'

'A few days ago a party of my men came across four dead companions of ours. One of them had that poster clutched in his dead hand. We do some business with the Comanches since, after all, you gringos stole their land, too, and we learned yesterday of their defeat at Jacob's Well. I spoke to a warrior who said they had recently captured this fellow Barton who promised to lead them to a large sum of money in return for his life. The Comanche have no use for money, and they handed him over to a trader called Gabriel.'

'So when we were spotted and our conversation overheard you started to put things together. You're no fool, Ortega, I'll say that for you.'

The Mexican pointed at him with his cigar. 'Neither are you, Señor Harrison. You killed those men, didn't you? It must have been you pursuing Barton for that reward money; how else could you have got mixed up in this?'

Harrison shrugged. 'What's that to you?'

'A man who can kill four of my best men single-handed is a man I could use on my side. You can fight but also have the sense to know when not to, so I'd like you to work for me. I'll pay you well — '

'As a matter of fact, I shot only three of those men and that was to save my own life. I catch outlaws but I'm not interested in becoming a hired killer.'

'You are interested in the woman though, Señora Sloane, are you not?' replied Ortega slyly. 'I can guarantee her safety if you agree to my proposition.'

Harrison leaned across the desk and looked straight into the Mexican's eyes. 'I'll defend her against any man who touches her and that includes you, Ortega.'

Ortega threw back his head and laughed. 'I don't doubt it; you're a man who does what he says he will do and I like that. I promise you that the lady will not be harmed and you'll still get the thousand dollars you're after. Perhaps then you will change your mind.'

'Well, don't count on it,' said Harrison as he stood up. 'If you want to get your hands on that strongbox, hadn't we better get going?'

'Of course. With luck we will reach the mine by noon tomorrow.'

When they stepped outside, Harrison's horse was waiting for him, a bandit holding the reins. The man handed him his guns as Ortega told him, 'I think I can trust you not to shoot me in the back. Besides, you might be needed if there's trouble.'

As they both mounted, Harrison noticed a tall young man, dressed entirely in black, talking to Coley. 'So, you slit the gringo officer's throat did you?' he heard him ask.

'That is my son, Jorge,' Ortega told him. 'His mother died giving birth to him and he has been causing me pain ever since. What is he up to now, eh?' He cantered ahead and spoke sharply to the young man in Spanish.

Jorge appeared to answer defiantly, whereupon Ortega struck him across the face with a pair of riding gloves. The younger man's hand flew up to his cheek and he cast a look of pure hatred at his father's retreating back as Ortega rode away. A small group of bandits gathered around him and they appeared to whisper animatedly before quickly breaking up to mount their own horses and ride off.

Ten outlaws, including Ortega and his son, had set off towards the mine. They expected to reach their destination by noon the following day. As they made their way through the canyon, Harrison caught up with Coley just as Jorge, who had been deep in conversation with him, rode on further ahead.

'What did Ortega want with you?' the corporal asked him.

'He wanted me to work for him, but I turned him down.'

Coley smiled. 'I'm glad to hear it, wouldn't want you to be on the wrong side.'

'Is that what you were talking to Jorge about, who's on what side?'

'It seems there's some bad blood between Jorge and his old man. Some o' the younger fellas want rid of Ortega and to put his son in charge. If young Jorge comes out on top, we could be in for a big share o' that money.'

'So how much is he paying you to slit his daddy's throat?' asked Harrison in disgust.

'It ain't like that,' protested Coley. 'He just wants to know who he can count on if the time comes.'

'Just leave me out of it.'

'OK, so long as you make sure them guns stay in their holsters.' With that, Coley rode on up ahead.

Harrison barely had time to gather his thoughts before Johnson rode up beside him.

'What's up with Coley?' he asked. 'It looked like you two were arguing.'

'It seems as though Jorge wants to take his father's place and Coley's eager to help.'

The sergeant shook his head. 'That boy's a damn fool. Gonna get hisself killed and us too if we ain't careful.'

'You're right there. Anyway, I told

him I wanted no part in it.'

'We'd best be on our guard and get ready to duck down if trouble starts.'

Harrison nodded. 'It's the lure of all that money. That's why Jorge is getting ready to make his move.'

'Yeah, I'm sorry I ever heard about it. That strongbox, it's the Devil's payroll, that's what it is. Everyone who goes after it ends up in a heap o' trouble.'

Harrison was not a superstitious man, but somehow it did seem as though the money was cursed in some way. He dismissed such thoughts from his mind as they journeyed out of the canyon and further across the desert. Ortega rode at the front, surrounded by a few of the older men, presumably close companions who had been with him a long time. Despite the oppressive heat, he did not slouch like the others but remained straight-backed in the saddle. Harrison could not help admiring the man's energy and determination; in different circumstances they might even have been friends. Glancing behind, he saw

Jorge riding next to Coley with Wilcox at the other side. They were accompanied by five of the younger bandits, the whole group talking among themselves and exchanging glances. Despite the heat, he shivered uneasily.

'Something's cookin' back there,' observed Johnson.

'We'll find out soon enough,' replied Harrison grimly.

Soon they were climbing as they reached a low-lying range and their pace slowed as they urged the horses up a steep path. Mountains rose up on each side of them as they hit higher ground and then the command came to halt. Harrison was curious about the delay and rode up to the front to find out what was happening, with Johnson following behind. Ortega and one of his companions had dismounted and were examining the remains of an abandoned wagon. Though covered in dust from its journey it was instantly recognizable as the one Gabriel had been driving.

Harrison jumped down to examine the tracks, which appeared quite fresh. Looking more closely he noticed a clump of uprooted sagebrush. Johnson followed his glance and got down beside him.

'Looks like they've been tryin' to cover their horse tracks after they cut 'em loose from the wagon,' remarked the sergeant. 'Why would they do that? We know where they're goin' anyway.'

Harrison glanced up at the surrounding cliffs. 'Perhaps they've taken a detour.'

No sooner had he spoken than a loud shriek echoed around them. Recognizing the attempted warning, he hurled himself against a startled Ortega, who had been standing perilously close to the foot of a nearby cliff. The two men rolled away as a huge boulder and rocks of all sizes cascaded towards them. Horses reared amid the clouds of dust and deafening roar of the avalanche. Two bandits who had been standing just feet away from Ortega were instantly buried. Another was struck on the shoulder and tumbled to his death down a gorge below them, while a fourth managed to dodge the falling rocks and steer his horse to safety. Slowly the dust settled and Harrison helped Ortega to his feet.

Gabriel's trap, probably set with Barton's connivance, allowed him to get further away from his pursuers, since it would take time to clear the rocks out of the way and tend to any wounded. However, Harrison had no doubt that the intention had been to kill them all, to eliminate any chance of being caught.

'You saved my life today. As a man of honour, I promise I shall not forget it,' said Ortega as he surveyed the damage surrounding them.

Harrison shrugged. 'You won't owe me anything as long as you abide by what we've already agreed. I'm sorry about your friends though.'

'They were good men, all of them loyal.' Ortega was watching Jorge approach with his companions as he added quietly, 'I fear that few such men remain.'

Johnson glanced up at the cliff above them. 'I guess Gabriel must ha' been up there waitin' for us, huh?'

'You guessed right, I think. Anyway, he'll get what he deserves when we catch up.'

Ortega sent two of his remaining men ahead to round up the horses that had fled while the rest of them cleared rocks away and buried the dead. Jorge and his companions did as they were told but reluctantly and with sullen looks. Three of his father's most trusted companions were dead, so the younger man was probably just biding his time.

'Those men you sent ahead to the mine, are they loyal?' Harrison asked Ortega.

The older man shrugged. 'Some perhaps, it's difficult to say. Jorge has been telling my men for some time now that I'm too old to lead them. My only chance is to appear strong, to be firm and decisive, even cruel sometimes.'

'Can't you talk to your son, reason with him?'

Ortega shook his head sadly. 'I am not a patient man but I have tried. He's always been wild, never respected me, so I demand obedience instead. Yet he's still my son.'

Then the two bandits returned with the horses and soon they were on their way again, making steady progress as the path sloped downwards and they emerged into open ground once more. The whole landscape seemed to glitter harshly in the sun's glare with just the occasional flash of colour as they passed cacti and other wild plants.

Johnson appeared lost in thought for a while, then he asked Harrison a question. 'Do you think that fella Gabriel findin' you in the desert, just turnin' up like that, coulda been more than a coincidence?'

'I don't see how,' Harrison replied, frowning.

'Well, it's just him pickin' you and

Mrs Sloane up, then Barton, who just happens to know where the money is, and gettin' the chance to take off like that seems kinda strange to me. The whole thing couldn't have gone better if he'd planned it, so maybe he did plan it.'

'I just assumed the man was an opportunist and took his chances when he found out about the money.'

Johnson nodded. 'Could be; just seems fishy to me, that's all.'

Harrison was disturbed by the man's words. After all, there was something strange about the whole thing, but Gabriel might not have seen them without Maggie flashing her mirror. Then he remembered her doing the same thing the previous day. Could she have been signalling to someone? Had she been in league with Gabriel all along? He shook his head. No, surely that could not be true! After all, he was certain it was her voice he had heard before the rocks hit them. Why would Maggie warn him if she had been deceiving him all along? Suddenly nothing seemed to make sense any more. Harrison was sure of one thing: he would get the answers he wanted once they reached that mine, whatever the cost.

6

They kept up a steady pace despite the heat, until Ortega ordered them to dismount for a while to give the horses a rest. After all, Gabriel and his companions would have to do the same if their animals were not to collapse from exhaustion. The men grumbled as they trudged wearily through the desert and Ortega berated them in Spanish. Harrison knew little of the language but enough to realize that the comparison made between their complaints and the behaviour of grandmothers and young children was not intended to be flattering. He noticed Jorge smile slyly and exchange remarks with Coley and one of the younger men, who grinned in response. Ortega tensed visibly but said nothing and their journey continued.

There was no water for several miles

according to Ortega's map, and their supplies were running low. They passed the skeleton of a horse and, a little further on, that of its rider. The bones were bleached white by the sun and seemed to offer a grisly warning of what might lie ahead. The atmosphere was tense and the party seemed to have split into two groups, one led by Ortega which included two older bandits, Johnson and Harrison, the other being led by Jorge and including his five followers, plus Coley and Wilcox. It was not to Harrison's liking but there it was and there was nothing he could do about it. At some point before they reached the mine, Jorge and his supporters would attack Ortega and the two older men. He and Johnson would have to decide what, if anything, they were going to do about it.

'Maybe we should just leave 'em all to it,' said Johnson, as if reading his thoughts.

'I'm not so sure we can afford to. Ortega has a code of honour, even if he is ruthless but if we stay neutral Jorge might decide that we're his enemies.'

'So what do we do?'

'We could help Ortega when the time comes and make it more of a fair fight.'

Johnson scratched his head. 'That puts me in one hell of a bind, havin' to fight men I've served with. It was me who gave Coley them corporal's stripes o' his; he was a good soldier once.'

'Look at Coley and Wilcox now, Sergeant. They're eaten up by greed, and if Jorge tells them to kill us to earn a share of that money then that's what they'll do.'

'Are you sure about that?'

Harrison sighed. 'I know men, I've seen what they're capable of, including the ones I thought decent. Come on, you went through the war; you know it too.'

'Yeah, I know,' whispered his companion hoarsely.

They were silent then, their mouths dry and their muscles weary as they stumbled onwards until at last they saw the creek ahead of them. Ortega announced that they would rest for thirty minutes after replenishing their water supplies as men and horses fell at the water's edge, drinking greedily.

Even alter resting however, the tension returned; every man was watchful, his hand ready to reach for his gun at the first sign of trouble. The moment finally came a few minutes before they were due to continue their journey.

'Hey, Ortega, we need longer to rest. We ain't goin' nowhere yet,' called Coley as he lounged by the creek.

The Mexican turned around angrily. 'Now you are a soldier in my army, we will be leaving as planned!'

Coley leaped to his feet as Jorge and the others gathered around behind him. 'You gonna make me?'

Ortega moved closer, then stopped and smiled. 'Very well, my friend, you can remain here but with no horse and no gun. How do you like that?'

Coley appeared nonplussed for a

moment. He was obviously trying to provoke a confrontation and get Ortega to draw his gun but the outlaw showed no sign of doing so. The outlaw leader then turned and spoke sharply to one of his companions who was about to reach for his weapon. He looked back at Coley and said, 'Come on, let's get going.'

Coley appeared to relax but his smile vanished as he suddenly went for his gun in one swift, fluid movement. Ortega was a fraction slower, now taken off guard, but Harrison was faster than either of them and the corporal had no chance to fire before a bullet ripped through his heart. Coley fell backwards into the creek with a splash, his eyes widening in surprise as the moment of death came. Harrison moved in an arc, a revolver in each hand. Two bandits at either side of Jorge fell to the ground as they each received a bullet, their own shots directed harmlessly upward. Johnson hit a third straight through the forehead before shooting

Jorge's gun from his hand. Jorge then dived between the horses to seek cover.

One of Ortega's companions was shot dead with a bullet in the throat and Ortega killed the young bandit responsible with a deadly throw of his knife before shooting the only bandit left among Jorge's supporters. Wilcox hit the old bandit to Ortega's left squarely in the chest, but Harrison returned his fire and blood seeped through the soldier's fingers as he fell forward, clutching his stomach. It was all over in less than a minute. Harrison was aware of a movement to his left and turned to see Jorge stumbling to his feet, his hands in the air.

With a cry of anguished rage, his father ran forward and pistol-whipped Jorge to the ground before kicking him repeatedly until the young man curled up into a tight ball in a vain attempt to protect himself. Ortega shouted curses in Spanish with each blow before he finally spat upon his son and turned away in disgust.

'I'd kill any other man who provoked this but . . . ' the Mexican shrugged as his words trailed away.

'There's been enough killing here today, just let him go,' suggested Harrison.

Ortega nodded. Johnson went over to Jorge and hauled him to his feet. 'Best get on a horse and get outta here,' he advised him, 'before we change our minds.'

'Tell him that if our paths cross again I'll kill him.' The old bandit kept his back to his son as he spat out the words.

'Did you hear that?' Johnson asked as Jorge wiped the blood from his mouth. The younger man nodded as he mounted his horse to ride away. Harrison watched his retreating back and wondered what would become of him, though briefly and without sympathy.

Silently, they buried the dead in shallow graves before mounting up to set off once more. Some of the dead men's horses had run off into the desert, startled by the gunfire but there were still a couple left, so Johnson and Harrison each took one to lead. No one spoke as they continued their journey, until Johnson spotted some tracks.

The sergeant mopped his brow wearily. 'It looks like three riders leadin' a horse behind passed by here not long ago. I guess we'd better press on 'til sundown if we don't wanna fall behind.'

Ortega nodded and continued to ride at the front, but now he slouched in the saddle, his face grey. He suddenly seemed like an old man, as though his son's treachery had sapped all the strength from his bones. They plodded on and were surprised to find themselves passing through what looked like a ghost town as the sun dipped slowly behind the horizon. There were rows of dilapidated, abandoned buildings to each side of them. Doors creaked on broken hinges and most of the windows had panes missing or were covered in dust. A light breeze blew a tumbleweed

102

ahead of them along the dusty street and the silence was eerie.

'This town must have been built because of the mine, there's nothing else within miles of the place,' remarked Harrison. 'When the silver ran out, there would have been no reason for it.'

'Do you think there's any whiskey left in the saloon?' asked Johnson hopefully.

Ortega's laugh sounded bitter. 'We could all use a drink, my friend.'

The saloon was round the next corner but, like the rest of the town, it looked as though it had been abandoned long ago. However, they were startled to hear sounds of laughter coming from inside and then a swarthy, bearded Mexican wearing a bandolier across his chest emerged through the swing back doors clutching a dusty bottle in one hand. He looked momentarily surprised to see Ortega but quickly recovered his composure.

'Ah, Don Pedro, you are here at last!' he cried as he came towards them.

'Lopez, your orders were to wait at

the mine and surprise Gabriel and his companions, so what are you doing here?' demanded Ortega sternly.

Apparently unperturbed by this rebuke, Lopez responded with a great belly laugh. 'We figured they would pass through here so we waited and gave them a little surprise this morning.' He tapped his forehead with a grimy finger and gave a knowing wink. 'You see, Don Pedro, a man of action must also be a man of brains.'

Ortega dismounted impatiently and seized the bottle from the bandit's hands. 'You won't keep your wits about you if keep drinking this stuff,' he said contemptuously. 'Where are your horses?'

'In the stables at the end of the street. It's a bit dusty, but they are all right.'

Ortega nodded. 'Very well, put our horses in there as well. Rub them down and give them some water.'

Lopez nodded reluctantly as Harrison and Johnson dismounted. 'Where are Jorge and the rest of the men?' he asked, looking suspiciously at his boss.

'Why, did you expect Jorge's little plot to succeed, eh? Are you sorry I'm not dead too?' Ortega towered over the man and Lopez sweated with fear, his eyes darting between the saloon, his boss and the companions who travelled with him, but he said nothing.

'Go on, get out of here!' Ortega told him contemptuously as the man scurried away.

Ortega led the way as they went inside to the sound of a tinkling piano. The saloon was covered in dust and cobwebs hung from the ceiling but that did not seem to bother the bandits sitting around the few tables that were left in the place. They had found some unopened bottles of brandy, rum and whiskey from which they sat swigging.

A nervous-looking man sat playing a piano that was badly in need of retuning. It was a moment before Harrison recognized Gabriel, as he had shaved off his beard and no longer wore spectacles.

'That's terrible, you must play better or I'll have to kill you,' said the red-shirted bandit who stood behind Gabriel wielding a pistol. To make his point, the man fired a shot into the wall opposite and the others joined in his laughter. Barton, his hands bound in front of him, sat drinking with the bandits while Maggie sat silently at one of the tables as she fended off the attentions of the drunken men at each side of her.

'What is this?' demanded Ortega. 'You should be on your guard. The time to celebrate is when we find the money, not before!'

The outlaw standing behind Gabriel gave a nonchalant reply. 'OK, just relax. We'll get the money tomorrow.'

'Don't tell me when to relax, Herrera. I give the orders here,' said Ortega coldly.

Herrera took another swig from the bottle beside him before wiping his long moustache with the back of his hand. He pointed his gun at Ortega. 'So, if you're still the boss where are all your men?' he asked insolently as he gestured with the weapon.

'Jorge is gone; there's no one else to lead you now.'

Herrera's leer of contempt vanished as he pointed his gun at Ortega's chest, the hammer thumbed back and ready to fire.

Ortega's knife caught him squarely in the throat and he staggered backwards, dropping his gun to the floor. There was a gargling noise as blood spurted from the wound and poured over his shirt front before he finally collapsed. Two of his companions reached for their guns but quickly put their hands up when Harrison drew his own weapons.

Ortega looked at each of the remaining four bandits in turn. 'Does anyone else want to challenge me? There was no reply but they all exchanged nervous glances.

'You are not men, you are cattle,' said their leader in disgust.

At that moment Lopez returned from

the stables. His eyes widened in horror when he saw Herrera's corpse lying in a pool of blood and he looked questioningly around the room.

'You wanted him to kill me, now you can bury him,' said Ortega, pointing at the two men who had reached for their weapons. Silently, they rose and dragged the dead Herrera outside. Curtly, Ortega instructed the remaining two bandits to take Barton away and lock him in the disused jail. Lopez did not wait for any orders but followed them as they went outside.

'I'll leave you to settle your scores,' Ortega told Harrison before he too left the saloon.

'Shall I stick around?' asked Johnson.

Harrison nodded but did not take his eyes off Gabriel, who coolly returned his stare.

'I'm a Pinkerton's man, working under cover for the army to recover their loot, so running out on you like that was nothing personal. I was just doing my job.'

'What about forcing Maggie to go along with you and then trying to kill me? Was that just doing your job?'

'He didn't force me, John. I agreed to help in return for a reward when he came to Brandon after Joel was killed, but everything else I've told you is true, I swear it.'

Gabriel defended her. 'Look Harrison, we needed you to get Barton to lead us to the money,' he said. 'He would only have agreed to do that if he thought he was going to get his hands on some of it. Unlike you, Maggie only did what she had to.'

'What's that supposed to mean?' demanded Harrison.

Gabriel sat back in his chair. 'It means that if you lie down with dogs you can expect to catch fleas. No one forced you to keep coming after that money or to get yourself mixed up with bandits and army deserters. That's why I started throwing rocks down at you and your unsavoury friends. I'm standing for the law here, so don't start getting sanctimonious.'

Johnson cut in before Harrison could reply. 'We were captured by those *bandidos* ourselves after comin' out here to get that payroll back for the army. Mr Harrison just wanted to get the reward for Barton and rescue Mrs Sloane because he thought you'd kidnapped her.'

Gabriel shifted awkwardly in his seat. 'Well, in that case I guess I owe you an apology, but my job's not over until that money is returned to its rightful owners.' He began stuffing tobacco into a hornrimmed pipe and struck a match against the table to light it. 'Barton and these folk don't know I'm a detective, which may just give us an edge.'

'You're assuming we'll help you, but that's a lot to take for granted,' said Harrison.

Gabriel nodded, blowing smoke into the air. 'I guess it is.' He pointed the stem of his pipe at Johnson. 'What about you, Sergeant?'

'I'm with you, but the bandits won't

give up that money without a fight.'

Harrison remained unsure. 'You were very convincing as a huckster, Gabriel. How do any of us know this isn't just another act to help you get your own hands on that money?'

Gabriel shook his head sadly. 'You're quite a cynic, aren't you? My official papers are sewn into the lining of my jacket but Maggie has seen them and can vouch for me.'

'He's telling the truth, John,' Maggie urged him. 'Come on, I know you were never really keen on sharing stolen money and now you've got the chance to do the right thing.'

Harrison nodded his agreement as he sat down. 'So, do you have a plan in mind?'

The detective drew on his pipe. 'We'll wait until it gets dark, then you go with Johnson to fetch Barton and bring him to the stables. I'll be there with Maggie and we'll let the other horses out so they can't follow us when we ride off.'

'It won't be easy takin' care o' the

guards and then gettin' away,' Johnson pointed out.

'No one said anything about it being easy, Sergeant. You'll have to knock out, maybe kill the guards and then we might have to shoot our way out.'

'Wait a minute. Have you got any of that laudanum left?' Harrison asked.

'Just a little, why?' Gabriel fumbled in his pocket for the bottle.

'We could bring Barton's guards some coffee. A few drops of that stuff and they'll soon be snoring. At least then we won't have to make any noise when we get him out.'

'Hmm, it might just work, but we'll only get one chance. Otherwise we're all dead.'

'I have no doubt of that.'

The voice was unmistakeably Ortega's and all eyes turned to look at him as he strode through the swing-back doors of the saloon and came towards them. He was alone and made no effort to draw his pistol, but he held a gunbelt in his hand, which he tossed on to the table.

'Yours, I believe,' he told Gabriel. 'I think you might need it.'

'How long have you been outside?' Harrison asked him.

'Long enough to hear everything.'

'It looks like you're figurin' on helpin' us, but why?' asked Johnson.

Ortega smiled. 'Come, Sergeant, you've seen my men. Which one of them would you trust?' He smiled when there was no reply. 'That is my point. Once that money is found, those dogs will shoot me in the back and then they'll start killing each other over who gets the biggest share.' Ortega shook his head. 'I want to make sure they don't see a cent.'

Gabriel nodded. 'Fine. They won't, but where does that leave you?'

'In a small house in Mexico where what I have saved will be enough to live on.'

'It sure feels good for us all to be on the right side of the law,' remarked Johnson. He paused before adding slyly, 'We'll all have the same empty pockets, just like honest folk.'

They all laughed at that but the tension remained. They might all be dead before morning.

7

'Forget the coffee idea; my men would prefer more whiskey, I'm sure,' said Ortega as he sat down at the table to join them.

'Yeah, I could bring some along, act friendly and get 'em to drink it,' added Johnson.

Harrison looked over the half empty bottles left by the outlaws earlier when Ortega sent them out. Three contained whiskey and there was an empty earthenware jug into which he tipped all of them. Gabriel poured in the last of the laudanum and the concoction was ready. However, it was Maggie who picked up the jug and turned towards the door.

'Wait a minute! This is far too dangerous for you. Johnson said he'd go,' protested Harrison. She gently prised his hand from her wrist but then patted it reassuringly. 'They won't suspect anything if I just go in there alone. Men like them think that women are good for only one thing, so they'll just relax and get drunk.'

'That's what worries me, Maggie. You won't be able to fight off two of them at once,' he warned her.

'They won't stay awake long enough to try anything, but you can hide outside if you think I might need help.'

'That's a good idea. Besides, Barton won't be easy to handle once he's outside that cell, so maybe Johnson should come along too.'

The sergeant nodded as he got to his feet. 'Let's go.'

Gabriel looked at his pocket watch. 'We'll meet you at the stables in two hours. That should be long enough.'

Outside, it was a clear night. The moon was almost full and the blue black-sky was filled with stars. On any other occasion Harrison would have enjoyed the spectacle but for now he was just grateful to be able to see where he was going. The jailhouse was at the other end of the street and they crept along behind the main buildings to avoid being spotted by any lookouts. At last they reached their destination and the two men crouched below a window that allowed them a clear view into the room. Maggie went inside, smiling at the two bandits guarding Barton as she held up the jug. Harrison watched as she pulled up a chair and offered them the drugged whiskey. They both drank greedily, passing the jug between them as they laughed at their good fortune. One of them picked up a small guitar that had been lying beside him and began to pluck the strings as he sang what sounded like a Mexican love song. His companion joined in while Maggie smiled encouragingly and clapped her hands in time to the music, frequently prompting the two guards to have another drink. Barton sat sullenly in his cell as he watched what was going on but said nothing.

Time passed, the men's voices

became slurred and one of them fell into a slumber. The other was still alert enough to start feeling suspicious when unable to rouse his companion. He swore and hurled the jug against the wall where it smashed. Maggie backed away as he fumbled for his gun but Harrison and Johnson were through the door in seconds.

'Put your hands up and turn around!' shouted Harrison as the guard stared at the revolvers that were pointed at him. The man did as he was told while Johnson removed his keys and gunbelt, unlocked the cell, then clubbed him over the back of the head with the butt of his gun. Barton moved towards the door and Harrison thumbed back the hammer on his revolver, shaking his head as a warning. Johnson dragged both outlaws inside the cell while Harrison kept Barton covered until they were ready to let him out. The cell was then locked and the keys thrown out of the window.

Johnson gave Barton a shove. 'C'mon, get movin', but no tricks, understand?'

'Them Mexicans were gonna kill me for sure, once they got their hands on that money, but how do I know I'll be better off with you fellas?' the outlaw asked.

'You don't,' Harrison told him, poking a pistol into his ribs, 'but if you make a run for it, you won't live to share that money with us.'

They stepped out into the moonlight and made their way towards the stables as quickly as they could. They saw no one and all was eerily quiet as they reached the other end of the street. Ortega was outside when they reached the stable door. 'I told the two men I posted as lookouts to get some rest,' he explained. 'By the time our noise wakes anyone up it should be too late for them to stop us.'

They slipped inside to find that Gabriel had their horses saddled and ready to go. He untied those belonging to the bandits and opened the doors wide. Barton was tied on to his mount, to be led behind Harrison, and then

Gabriel swung himself into the saddle of a dappled mare. He raised his pistol and fired it three times in quick succession. The bandits' horses galloped off into the night, closely followed by the fugitives making their escape. Bleary-eyed bandits stumbled from their bedrolls as Harrison and his companions raced out of the ghost town. A couple of shots were fired in their direction but no one was hit and soon they were well on their way.

They kept riding for a couple of hours, then Ortega suggested that they should rest until dawn. Johnson lit a fire and they bedded down for some much needed rest while Harrison took the first watch, mainly to prevent Barton making any attempt at escape. He sat wrapped in a blanket, watching the stars, but his gun was in his lap and he remained alert for any sound. The time passed uneventfully before Ortega came over to replace him. Within minutes he was asleep but in his dreams he chased piles of dollars whipped up by the wind.

The faster he ran, the further they flew away from him while the mocking laughter of the gods echoed in his mind. Harrison awoke with a start as the first streaks of dawn appeared in the sky, hoping that his nightmare did not turn out to be an evil omen of some kind.

The mingled smells of coffee and frying eggs brought a change in his mood. Maggie had prepared them a fine breakfast but they ate quickly, keen to get on their way. They kept up a steady pace and as noon approached Johnson pointed out a row of ramshackle wooden huts just ahead of them. As the disused winding shaft came into view it was clear that this was the place, and they slowed their horses to a trot.

'All right, Barton, where is it?' asked Gabriel.

The outlaw dismounted and walked over to the entrance to a limestone cave near the winding shaft. Turning, he looked around, frowning for a moment, then he stopped by a low, rather flat boulder. Holding out his bound hands he said, 'It's under here.'

Ortega drew a short spade from his saddle-bag and threw it down, then dismounted and cut Barton's bonds with his knife. 'You'd better start digging,' he told him. The stone was quickly shoved aside and Barton set about his task. As he dug deeper, he became excited and by the time his spade struck metal he could hardly contain himself.

'It's here! It's here!' he cried. He went down on his knees in the pit he had dug and hauled the strongbox out as the others all gathered around in a circle.

Barton looked up at them all pleadingly. 'I know we gotta share but can I be the first to open it?'

Gabriel shrugged. 'I don't see why not; you put it there in the first place.'

The lock had been shot away when Barton originally buried the box and all he had to do was lift the lid. No one saw the Colt .45 that lay on top of the cash as he kept the lid tilted towards him when he started firing. The first bullet hit Gabriel in the stomach and as the Pinkerton's man was spun around by the impact the second one hit Ortega squarely between the eyes. The third shot would have been for Harrison but he was already firing back with both guns, aiming low shots into the pit as Johnson reached for his weapon too.

Three bullets hit Barton squarely in the chest and he fell back into the hole he had just dug, but Harrison kept firing into the outlaw's twitching, bloodstained body until he had emptied both chambers. Then, as his rage subsided, he turned his attention to the victims.

Ortega lay on his back, his eyes staring blankly at the sky. Harrison knelt down beside him and gently closed them. Maggie and Johnson were both tending to Gabriel, who was still alive. Harrison fetched him some water and pulled the detective's coat aside to examine his wound. A stain was rapidly spreading across his stomach as blood pooled on the ground beside him. Maggie cradled his head in her lap and wiped the sweat from his deathly pale features with her handkerchief as Johnson tried in vain to stanch the wound. Gabriel took a sip from the canteen Harrison offered him and then coughed hoarsely. His voice was thin and reedy as he whispered to them. 'It's no use. I'm not going to make it.'

There was a desperate urgency in his rasping tone as Gabriel tried to continue. 'Get the money . . . Fort Concho . . . Grierson . . . ' He stopped for a moment as his breathing became more laboured, and then gripped Harrison's lapel with surprising strength. He opened his mouth to speak again but the words died in his throat as he breathed his last in a long sigh.

'Did that make any sense to either of you?' Harrison asked his companions.

'Colonel Grierson's our commanding

officer over at Fort Concho. I guess he would be the best person around here to take charge of the money,' Johnson told him. 'There's a town there, place called San Angela. We head west and follow a trail through the Pecos Mountains. It'll take us a few days to reach it though.'

Maggie laid a hand on Harrison's arm. 'It could be very dangerous, John. There'll be outlaws and Comanches hiding out there.'

'That's why you're going to wait for us over the border somewhere safe.'

'No! Damn it, John, I can take care of myself and I can shoot pretty straight too!'

'I don't doubt it but there's no need — '

'There's every need! It'll be much safer with three of us and you know it. You might as well give in now. I'll only follow you anyway.'

Johnson chuckled as Harrison let out a sigh. 'If you two don't quit arguin' like that you'll have to get married.'

Maggie flushed red and looked down while Harrison picked up the shovel and busied himself digging a grave for Gabriel. Johnson pitched in and soon all the bodies were buried. They left Barton until last and used the pit in which he had hidden the cash as it seemed fitting, somehow. The strong-box contained paper money in wads of a $1,000 each which they divided up into equal piles and put into six small sacks they found in Gabriel's saddle-bag. They watered their horses at a small creek near by, refilled their canteens and set off again across the baking desert, Johnson leading the way.

The Tenth Cavalry had only moved over to Fort Concho that year but Johnson already knew the territory well. As the afternoon wore on the sun settled over the peaks of the Pecos Mountains and all seemed peaceful, but Johnson warned them to remain on their guard. Harrison's hooded eyes scanned the horizon, but he saw no signs of any danger and he relaxed slightly. The Comanches had no overall leader and were divided into many different bands. Not all had been defeated or settled on reservations and Harrison could not help admiring their spirit of resistance. Their lands had been taken and the spread of cattle ranching had almost obliterated their way of life. He could not blame them for fighting back.

It was late afternoon when they reached the start of the trail through the mountains that would eventually lead them to Fort Concho. On an escarpment high above, two men looked down on the tiny figures below. The elder of them peered through a telescope and described what he saw. 'There are three of them. The one in front is a black but looks like a soldier. Then a gringo, dressed fancy, and a woman.' His gaze lingered for a moment on Maggie Sloane and he grinned, showing a number of gold teeth.

'Let me see, Pablo, it could be them,' whispered Jorge urgently. His companion passed him the telescope and he peered through it eagerly. 'Yes, that's the sergeant in front with Harrison behind and she must be that Sloane woman.' Jorge lowered the telescope slightly. 'They're carrying mailbags, so they've got the money. Quick, give me a rifle.'

Pablo placed a restraining hand on the younger man's arm. 'You could easily miss them from here and then they get a warning about us.'

'We can't just let them get away!' protested Jorge.

Pablo paused to scratch his greying beard. 'Jorge, my friend, you must learn to be more patient. That gringo Harrison is fast with the guns, no? I saw the graves when you took me to the old mine, which explains why only three are left.' Pablo looked thoughtful for a moment. 'We should keep following but stay out of sight. There are only the two of us, after all.' He grinned again as he turned back to Jorge. 'It was good luck you running into me, no?'

The orange sun dipped below the mountains as dusk fell. Wearily, Harrison and his companions made camp for the night. Harrison stretched out his aching limbs on a bedroll and looked across at Maggie, who was sitting up to take the first watch. He found himself thinking of her as he drifted off to sleep, hoping somehow that whatever his future held, she would be a part of it.

They were all up as the first streaks of dawn appeared in the sky, their movements observed by the two bandits high above them.

'We could make things less risky for ourselves and more unpleasant for them,' suggested Jorge. 'See how they unpacked everything. They sleep with their mailbags close to them but the other things were piled up together just at the edge of the camp.'

The older man nodded and a grin spread across his swarthy features as Jorge described what he intended to do that night.

'That's very clever, *amigo*. Then, when they are weak, we will attack.'

8

Harrison remained on edge throughout the day. He was somehow sure that they were being watched and he kept glancing up at the surrounding peaks for signs of movement. Once or twice he was sure he saw something but could not be sure.

'I know what you're thinking,' Johnson told him. 'There are paths up there where you could hide a column of infantry. If there are any bandits up there we won't see them.'

'There can't be many. Otherwise they'd just attack us instead of skulking around.'

Maggie shivered despite the heat. 'The sooner we get to Fort Concho the better.'

'I reckon it should take about three days.'

'Unless we run into more trouble,' added Harrison.

They met no one on the road,

although some worn tracks suggested a wagon train had passed along that way a few days before. The recent hostilities with the Comanche and Kiowa tribes as well as the activities of outlaws had made the area more dangerous, despite the existence of several forts to ensure the safe passage of travellers and their goods.

'I wonder if old Fire-face Kinsella's around here someplace?' said Johnson at length.

'Isn't he that officer who's been out here chasing Indians?' asked Maggie.

'Yeah, Captain Sean Kinsella. He sure is one mean dog but I'd like to run into him, anyhow. We'd be safe with him around.'

Harrison smiled to himself. Johnson's description was an apt one since Kinsella had a reputation not only for courage and competence but also for intolerance of any dissent. The man was a formidable opponent both on and off the field: one they could do with on their side in the present circumstances.

For the moment, however, they were alone in the desert and responsible for the safe return of $100,000 in stolen money. It was a sobering thought.

As dusk fell once more they approached a cave and were glad of the opportunity to enjoy some shelter. Jorge and Pablo smiled as they observed them disappear inside. It would soon be time to carry out their plan.

Harrison piled up the saddle-bags near the mouth of the small cave, allowing everyone more space to stretch out, but they each kept a couple of mailbags stuffed with dollars beside them as they settled down to sleep. Maggie volunteered to stay on watch for a couple of hours before waking Harrison to take over. Johnson was already snoring as she tried to make herself comfortable with a blanket around her shoulders and a rifle across her knees. After an hour she felt herself begin to doze but then she suddenly sat up with a start. Maggie was sure she had heard something, a faint rustling. Peering into the darkness, she thought she saw a shape move; she went over to the mouth of the cave to look outside. There was no one there and though her ears were straining she could not hear a sound. Shaking her head, she sat down again and silently cursed her vivid imagination.

Harrison awoke as the first light of dawn filtered into the cave. Rubbing his eyes, he sat up slowly. His mouth was dry and his tongue felt like sandpaper. The others were stirring as he searched among their baggage for a canteen of water. Harrison found what he was looking for but frowned in puzzlement when he discovered that it was empty. On turning it over, he noticed a slit in the side of the container, which looked as though it had been made with a knife. Underneath were two more, both empty and each with a similar hole through which the water had seeped away. He knew there was another bottle but was unable to find it though he continued to search frantically.

Maggie came over to join him. 'What

are you looking for?' she asked sleepily. Silently, he handed her the damaged canteens.

'I really did hear something after all,' she muttered, 'but I can't understand why anyone would do this. It doesn't make any sense.'

'It makes perfect sense,' Harrison told her. 'We won't last long out here without any water. It will be much easier to rob us once we're too weak to put up a fight.'

'We have got some water left.' They turned around as Johnson held up the missing canteen. 'I had it by me last night, but what's left won't last long.'

There was a long, uneasy silence as they each pondered what to do next. Then, suddenly, each heard the sound of hoofs in the distance, getting louder as they rapidly approached. Without a word, they all ran to the mouth of the cave.

'Well, ain't that a fine sight to see, Mr Harrison? That there's the cavalry!' Johnson was jumping up and down in excitement.

'Are you sure? I can't see their uniforms yet, just a cloud of dust.'

'Yeah, I can just make out the formation.'

'Really?' Maggie asked Johnson excitedly, hardly daring to believe their luck.

'I've never been surer of anything,' he told her.

As the cloud came nearer, Harrison saw that the riders were nearly all 'buffalo soldiers', wearing blue tunics beneath the layer of dust which enfolded them. Johnson waved at the approaching column and the red bearded officer in command slowed his men to a halt.

'Sergeant Eli Johnson, sir, of B Company, Tenth Cavalry.'

The officer acknowledged his salute. 'Captain Sean Kinsella. This is D Company from the Ninth. What are you doing out here?'

Johnson gave an edited version of their adventures: one in which Schmidt, Coley and Wilcox had all died bravely at the hands of the outlaws before the rest of them escaped and located the stolen money. 'Sir, I thought it was best to get along to Fort Concho and hand the money over to Colonel Grierson, seein' as it was him who hired Mr Gabriel to get it back for the army. Do I have your permission to proceed with the column?'

Kinsella nodded. 'Yes, we're on our way back there now.' He turned his watchful, grey eyes towards Harrison. 'I'm afraid your capture of Swift Eagle was in vain. The Comanches came back that night and launched another attack. They rescued him and killed about half the soldiers left before they were finally beaten off. We've been out here trying to hunt him down but . . . ' the captain shrugged as his words trailed off, but then he straightened up. 'Still, you did well finding that money, Sergeant. We're grateful to you too, Mr Harrison, and you, ma'am.'

'We're just glad the money's in safe hands now,' Maggie told him.

Kinsella ran his hand through a crop

of wavy red hair. 'Well, it will be once we get to the fort. So will you, ma'am, it's not safe for any of you out here at the moment. We haven't run into those Comanches but they'll be around here somewhere, I guarantee it.'

'Do you think they're likely to attack?' Harrison asked.

'Maybe, depends on how many there are. You three on your own would stand no chance against them, that's for certain.'

* * *

Jorge had always been a light sleeper and, hearing the approach of horsemen, he climbed down behind a boulder just above the cave. He heard enough to learn that Swift Eagle was free and that the soldiers had been looking for him. He knew of several places where the Comanches might be, since he had brought them guns and stolen horses many times in the past. Finding them would not be too difficult, but Harrison

137

and his companions were now protected by about fifty soldiers. What might persuade Swift Eagle to attack them when the odds were not very favourable? He thought he might have the answer to that problem.

Jorge returned to their camp to find Pablo still snoring. He shook him awake. 'We have to get moving,' he told his companion and hurriedly packed their things away.

'Why, what's the big rush?'

Jorge told Pablo about Kinsella's arrival. 'Our three friends now have a cavalry escort to Fort Concho, so we can forget about attacking them today.'

'Damn, we'll never see that money now.' The older man spat contemptuously.

'Don't be so sure. Those blue bellies are out here hunting the Comanches who attacked that trading station a few days ago. I used to trade with them, so they've had a lot of horses and guns from me in the past.'

Pablo sat up, suddenly hopeful. 'Do they trust you?'

'Sure they do. If I tell them that Kinsella was boasting about how he was going to wipe them out, Swift Eagle will want to attack them first.'

Pablo grinned as he tossed his blanket aside and got to his feet. 'That's good, real good. They won't know what's hit them.'

Jorge grinned back. 'Then it will be tequila and *señoritas* for both of us eh?'

★ ★ ★

They were making steady progress along the trail. Johnson was in an ebullient mood now that he was back among fellow soldiers, Maggie felt safe and even Harrison was starting to relax. Perhaps their troubles really were at an end.

'What will you do after we give the money to Colonel Grierson?' Maggie asked him.

'I think I'd like to take up law again, but I'm not sure where. Richmond has painful memories, but I'm tired of hunting desperate men, of having to kill or be killed.'

'You're looking for a quiet place where you can be at peace,' she observed.

'Yes, I suppose I am. Do you know of anywhere?'

Maggie smiled wistfully. 'My two boys, Joshua and Ethan, are with my mother in San Antonio. It's a beautiful city and the house overlooks the main square. I don't know of any other place quite like it. That's where I'll be going.'

'Was your husband from San Antonio?'

Maggie's mouth twisted into a grimace. 'Joel had no roots anywhere. He was always dreaming that one day he'd make a heap o' money and he chased that dream wherever it took him 'til he ended up on the street in Brandon with Clay Barton's bullet in him.'

'I'm sorry. I didn't mean to rake up the past. I should have remembered that you're still grieving.' Harrison shifted uneasily in his saddle.

Maggie shook her head vigorously.

'No, I'm not. I got over him a long time ago, long before he died. Even our sons hated him, hated his drinking, his womanizing and his heavy hand with a belt. I only stayed with him out of fear, fear of what he might do if I tried to run away.' The words were spoken quietly but clearly and decisively.

'I'm so sorry, I had no idea.'

She turned to him then, her ocean blue eyes meeting his gaze. 'That's all right. I was just thinking that if San Antonio can bring me peace, it just might do the same for you.'

Harrison nodded slowly as he tried to appear nonchalant. 'Perhaps you're right. Maybe I'll just tag along and see what the place has to offer.'

★　★　★

It was nearly sundown by the time Jorge and Pablo found the Comanches' hideout. As they approached, four men seized them and bound their hands.

'You know me! I used to bring you

horses and guns!' Jorge protested, but the young warriors pushed them forward towards Swift Eagle's tepee, saying nothing in reply. The war chief came out as they drew near and eyed them both suspiciously in the fading light.

'I bring you news of your enemies. Do you want to hear it?' Jorge asked him.

Swift Eagle nodded curtly. 'Speak.'

'Today I saw fifty buffalo soldiers led by a man called Kinsella. They are looking for your camp and hope to destroy you. The man who captured you at Jacob's Well, Harrison, is with them and also the soldier who helped him. This is Pablo. He too is a friend of the Comanche and comes to bring you this warning.'

Swift Eagle gestured to one of the guards and their bonds were cut. 'I know that there are soldiers. My scouts have seen their tracks. This Kinsella, does his face look like fire?'

Jorge thought for a moment, then he

remembered the officer's red beard. 'Yes, he does. The hair on his head is like that too.'

'I know he is fierce in battle. We must wait until more braves come before we fight.'

This was not the response they were hoping for. Pablo opened his mouth to speak but Jorge gestured to him to remain silent before he himself went on. 'I heard him say that he will destroy you and all your people. He travels to Fort Concho as we speak to get more men and guns.'

'Why do you come here to tell me this?'

'Harrison killed my men and took my money, but I need your help to kill him. If you wait, Kinsella will only get more soldiers and grow in strength.'

Swift Eagle nodded slowly as he took in the Mexican's words, then he handed him a stick. 'Show me where you saw them,' he demanded.

Jorge sketched the shape of the mountains in the dirt, the road with the location of the troops marked by a stick figure on horseback and a line from it tracing the route to the camp.

Swift Eagle spoke solemnly. 'We will attack Fire-face and his soldiers tomorrow. You will ride with us and take what is yours from Harrison.'

They both nodded their agreement, not caring that Swift Eagle had been deceived about Kinsella's intentions. Soon the two *bandidos* would be enjoying a life of luxury, far away from the Comanches and their battles with the army.

9

The sound of the bugle awoke him and Harrison tossed his blanket aside with a groan. Then he heard another sound, the thunder of galloping hoofs accompanied by a Comanche war cry. He turned and saw the rapidly approaching band of warriors mounted on their distinctive pinto horses. A figure in a horned buffalo-scalp helmet was among them; it could only be Swift Eagle, proudly wearing the headdress of a war chief. Half-dressed soldiers leaped to their feet, reaching for their weapons in panic as the first shower of arrows rained down upon them. Harrison saw one man aim with his pistol and then fall dead to the ground before he had even fired a shot. Others were also being hit, but Johnson and another sergeant were quickly getting the troops organized into groups and were directing their fire. Kinsella emerged from a tent, his tunic unbuttoned and a revolver in each hand as he shouted orders.

The Comanches were riding through the camp now, throwing spears and firing off arrows to the right and left of them. Every soldier was armed and firing back by this time, and a few warriors tumbled from their horses to the ground. Harrison joined the fight, shooting down three of them in quick succession as they rode towards him. The next few minutes were a blur of gunshots, painted faces and rearing hoofs as he continued firing while trying to get across to a supply wagon where he could take cover. He heard a scream from behind him and turned around to see a Comanche trying to pull Maggie on to his horse. Harrison aimed and squeezed his trigger but there was just an empty click. There was no time to reload and he set off at a sprint.

Fortunately, Maggie put up more of a fight than the warrior expected and he was leaning over in the saddle as she tried to pull away. Harrison leaped the last few feet and smashed into him with the full force of his weight. The horse stumbled and the Comanche was pulled to the ground as Maggie scrambled for safety. He was strong, however and sent Harrison sprawling with a hard punch. His eyes blazing, the buckskinned warrior drew his knife and moved in for the kill. Harrison looked around frantically for a weapon and then grabbed a saucepan from over a campfire just by him. The scalding contents caught his opponent in the face and his hands went up to his eyes as he screamed in pain. Now the knife was on the ground between them and Harrison seized his chance. He picked it up and plunged the blade into the Comanche's stomach, twisting it as he did so. He jumped over the crumpled body and found Maggie huddled by a tent, clutching a pistol.

'Come on, let's get you somewhere safe.' Taking her by the hand, he hurried over to the wagon and then dropped down behind it with her by his side. Quickly, he reloaded both his revolvers and then checked Maggie's weapon too. Peering around the side, he saw that the Comanches were now in retreat and the fighting had died down. Then, frowning, he noticed something else, or rather, *someone* else. It was Jorge! What was he doing here? He was on horseback, firing at soldiers with his revolver but he also appeared to be looking for something, his eyes scanning his surroundings. Harrison came out from behind the wagon and fired but his shot missed. The Mexican saw that his companions were in retreat and wheeled his horse around to gallop after them. Harrison fired after him but the bandit was now out of range and he cursed loudly.

'They're going, shouldn't we be pleased?'

'They'll be back, Maggie. The Comanches don't like to risk too many losses at once, so they'll return when they think they have the advantage again.'

Their conversation was interrupted as Kinsella approached them. 'That was good shooting, Mr Harrison. Are you both all right?'

'Yes, we're not injured,' Harrison told him. 'What are we going to do now?'

Kinsella stroked his beard thoughtfully. 'Ideally, I'd like to keep moving, but the trail narrows up ahead for the next few miles. If they attack us there we could be trapped. Our position here is easier to defend, though.'

'Is there anything I can do to help?'

Kinsella made a sweeping gesture with his arm. 'We're moving some of the wagons around to build a barricade. We could use an extra pair of hands to help with that.'

Harrison nodded. 'Consider it done.'

'Thanks. We'll need to move the water, food and ammunition supplies well behind the barricade so the Comanches can't get at them.'

'They'll probably try to chase off our horses as well.'

'You're right about that. I'll get some of the troop mounted to engage them, move the other horses further back and assign some men to guard them.'

It did not take long to organize the defences and Harrison was soon settled down behind one of the wagons with Johnson and a few other men. Maggie was with them, a box of ammunition by her side as she helped to check and load their weapons.

'Did you see our old friend Jorge out there with the Comanches?' Johnson asked.

'I took a shot at him but missed.'

'That's a shame. He won't quit 'til he gets his hands on that money. I saw another Mexican with 'em too, an older fat fella. He could be in this too.'

'There's not much they can do if we fight them off,' said Maggie.

Johnson shook his head. 'I wouldn't be so sure about that. They'll hook up with some other gang if they have too. Jorge don't know when to quit.'

'I wonder if they were the ones who stole our water?' she replied.

Harrison rubbed his chin. 'That would make sense. I'll be watching out for Jorge and his sidekick when they come back.'

The Comanches had regrouped a couple of miles away. 'The fire faced one fought well,' observed Swift Eagle. 'Nine braves were killed.'

'They lost far more,' said Jorge encouragingly. 'Your next attack will destroy them.'

'They will be ready. They have the wool hair and dark skin of the buffalo. They are fierce when they have been angered.'

'You are right, Swift Eagle, but you have always hunted the buffalo, no? You can hunt these ones too. I saw our enemy, Harrison. He hides behind them and laughs at us.'

'You must learn patience in battle. We will attack when it is time.'

Their conversation was interrupted by a scream. One of the soldiers had been captured and lay bound and stripped to the waist as a warrior applied a heated knife to his skin. Pablo stood watching with interest.

'You could humble Kinsella and Harrison without attacking them,' Jorge suggested.

Swift Eagle frowned. 'How can this be?'

'They are carrying bags of money to Fort Concho. Tell them they will not be attacked if they give this money up. If they obey out of fear, you will have shamed them.'

Swift Eagle shook his head. 'Fire-face will not obey.'

Jorge shrugged. 'Then you can attack him anyway.'

Swift Eagle nodded his assent and Jorge dropped down on one knee beside their captive. A layer of flesh had been removed from his forearm and he was grimacing with pain.

'Listen, *amigo*. We will spare your life if you take this message to Kinsella. If he gives up the money he is carrying, there will be no more fighting. Otherwise you will all die. Harrison must bring the money here by sundown and he must come alone.'

The soldier nodded weakly and was cut loose before being pulled to his feet by Pablo and helped on to a horse. The two outlaws watched him canter away. 'Once I have the money, I will crush Harrison like a worm,' Jorge muttered.

His companion nodded approvingly. 'That's right, *amigo*. A man's gotta know how to hate his enemies.'

★ ★ ★

The tension was mounting as Kinsella and his men awaited the next attack. They were all on edge, straining their ears to hear the pounding of hoofs or a distant war cry, but there was only silence. Then a lone rider approached and as he came nearer Harrison saw that he slouched in the saddle. Kinsella came running forward as a guard seized the horse's bridle and steadied its rider, who seemed on the point of collapse.

'It's Corporal Burgess, sir. It looks

like he's been hurt pretty bad.'

Kinsella lifted the man down himself and carried him over to a tent which was being used to treat the wounded. Harrison watched as they disappeared inside and began to wonder why the Comanches had released him.

'I dread to think what they did to that poor man,' said Maggie, shaking her head.

'He's lucky he ain't dead. The Comanches are sending a message,' Johnson told her.

A few minutes later Kinsella emerged from the tent and strode towards them. 'Mr Harrison, come with me please. This concerns you.'

Harrison followed the officer into the tent where he saw Burgess lying unconscious on a bench. An orderly was tending his left arm from which almost half the skin had been burned away. 'Before he passed out, the corporal gave me a message from a Mexican who was riding with the Comanches. You're to bring that payroll money, alone, to them by sundown or they'll attack again. Do you know this man?'

'Jorge Gonzales-Ortega is the son of the bandit leader Johnson told you about. He knows about the money and he's manipulating the Comanches' grievances in order to get it.'

Kinsella shook his head. 'We can't give in to blackmail but if there's some way we can fool them, would you be willing to help?'

'If it will save lives, certainly. Where are the Comanches now?'

'Burgess said they're about two miles away on a slope above the trail. They can see what's coming and it's a steep climb to get up there, so there's no point trying to attack.'

Harrison thought for a moment. 'Do you have any gunpowder?'

'We keep some in the supply wagon. It comes in handy sometimes.'

'Good. This is what I suggest we do.' Harrison outlined his plan as Kinsella listened.

'You're taking a big risk but it might

just work. I'd send someone with you but that would only make them suspicious.'

Harrison nodded. 'I understand, Captain.' Then he handed the officer his pocket watch. 'If I don't come back, please give this to Maggie Sloane.'

The preparations did not take long and he was ready to leave within an hour. As he finished loading the pack-horse he heard a voice behind him.

'Weren't you going to say goodbye?'

He turned to face her. 'I'll come back soon, Maggie. There's nothing to worry about.'

She shook her head. 'Whatever you're doing, it must be dangerous. Please be careful.'

'I will,' Harrison assured her. 'Now get back behind those wagons where it's safe.'

Johnson appeared as she turned to go. 'I figure you might need some help.'

'I appreciate it and there's no one else I'd rather have to guard my back, but this is something I have to do

156

alone.' As the sergeant opened his mouth to protest he added, 'That's an order from Captain Kinsella.'

'Good luck,' said Johnson, extending a hand towards him.

'Thanks. If I don't come back, it's been good to know you.' He shook the sergeant's hand warmly, then swung himself into the saddle and rode out to meet the Comanches.

Jorge peered through his telescope as the rider approached, leading a pack-horse behind him. 'It's Harrison. See how he hurries to his death.' He passed the instrument to Pablo on his left while Swift Eagle stood beside him on the right, watching impassively.

'If he has brought the white man's money, it is enough. He is not to be harmed.' The Comanche spoke sharply. 'We keep our promises. They are not broken like treaties.'

The two outlaws nodded reluctantly. At least they would have $100,000 to spend. Jorge watched as Harrison drew to a halt. 'Unload the bags and open them!' he called.

Harrison carried the three mailbags he had brought with him to the foot of the cliff and untied the knot at the top of each one. Jorge examined them through the telescope and smiled as he spotted the wads of cash. Then something unexpected happened. The bounty hunter stood back from the cliff and called out, 'Swift Eagle! Come down, I want to talk to you.'

'Don't listen to that gringo, it's a trick!' hissed Jorge.

Harrison opened his coat. 'Look, I'm unarmed. Please, I just want to talk.'

Ignoring Jorge's protestations, the Comanche dismounted and climbed nimbly down to the path below. When he arrived Harrison dismounted and the two men faced each other.

'Tell me, what made you decide to attack the column?' Harrison asked.

'Our friends told us that Fire-face was here with his men to hunt us down and destroy us, but you know this, you were with them.'

Harrison casually lit a cigar and drew on it. 'It is true that Captain Kinsella had been looking for you, but when you attacked the column he'd given up and was on his way back to Fort Concho. Jorge and his friend have been lying to you.'

Swift Eagle stiffened. 'I only know of white men's lies. Why should I believe you?'

Harrison pointed to the sacks with his cigar. 'Look underneath that money.'

The Comanche's eyes narrowed with suspicion but he did as he was asked and then gasped with surprise. 'You have brought the black powder that brings destruction. Why?'

'I was supposed to drop this cigar against the bottom of one of those sacks and blow you all up but I just couldn't bring myself to do it.'

Swift Eagle folded his arms. 'Were you afraid, Harrison?'

'No, it wasn't that. I fight when I have to defend myself but I don't want to destroy your people. I don't care about that money and I know you don't. Who does?'

The Comanche thought for a moment. 'The army, Jorge and Pablo do.' He nodded slowly. 'I have seen the greed in their eyes when they speak of it.'

'Why not let them fight the army for it if they want to? I promise you, let us go in peace and you will not be hunted.' Then he handed Swift Eagle the cigar.

'You risked death rather than destroy us,' said the Comanche. 'I might have killed you when I saw the black powder.' He dropped the cigar and ground it into the dirt. 'For what you have done today I will do as you ask. Tell Fire-face there can be peace between us.' Then he turned and climbed back up the cliff.

Harrison put the bags back on to the pinto, mounted it and rode back towards the camp. Maggie was the first to reach him and flung herself into his arms as he dismounted. They held each other tightly for a moment as she buried her head in his shoulder. He released her as the men swarmed around him, clapping and cheering. Then the crowd parted and fell silent as Kinsella approached to shake him warmly by the hand. He paused when he noticed the unused sacks of gunpowder.

'Would you care to explain this, Mr Harrison?'

'I just couldn't do it, so I took a chance instead. Swift Eagle only attacked the column because he thought you were going to hunt him and his people down. Once he realized he had been deceived he was willing to make peace.'

Kinsella snorted with disgust. 'Make peace indeed! Have you forgotten what his people did at Jacob's Well? How do you know he won't just attack us anyway? You had a chance to get rid of that menace and you just threw it away!'

'If that's true, why did he let me go? Swift Eagle could have killed me but he didn't.'

The officer shrugged. 'You risked your life in an effort to make peace, I acknowledge that, but you had no right to risk the lives of my men. If the

161

Comanches attack us again, let it be on your conscience.' With that he turned and walked away. These Southerners were a strange breed and Kinsella was not sure he would ever understand them, even if he spent the rest of his life in Texas.

★ ★ ★

Jorge had been amazed to see Harrison get back on his horse and ride off with the money. He had no idea what the bounty hunter had said to Swift Eagle but it had clearly worked. When the Comanche returned his features were set in a grimace.

'You go now. There is no truth in what you have told us.'

The *bandidos* tried to protest. 'Come, Swift Eagle, the gringo is trying to deceive you. I am your friend who has brought you guns and horses — '

'No, you have sold us guns and horses. Now you try to use us to get the white man's dollars. I warn you and this fat one. Leave now or we will kill you!'

Seeing that their lives were now in danger, the two *bandidos* turned and rode away without another word. They continued in silence for a while until Jorge remembered the town attached to Fort Concho. San Angela was a rough place, full of saloons and whorehouses which suited the plan that was beginning to form in his mind. They were certain to need more help and desperate men would rob and kill on the promise of even a few hundred dollars.

'When they get that money to Fort Concho it will be put somewhere safe,' he said.

'So what?' There was a sour edge to Pablo's tone. 'We won't be able to get at it.'

'I wouldn't be so sure of that. The money won't be being moved all the time, or be constantly under the guard of fifty men. If we keep our eyes and ears open, we might get to find out where it is.'

His companion thought for a moment.

'I have a cousin in San Angela who has a saloon. Some of the soldiers go in there.'

'There, you see! You were ready to give up too easily, *amigo*. With just a few of the right men, we might be able to break in and steal that money after all.'

'Once my cousin helps us to find out where it is,' Pablo reminded him.

'Of course. You can always loosen tongues in a saloon, no?'

Pablo smiled, showing his gold teeth. 'Yes, with plenty tequila and plenty *señoritas*.'

★ ★ ★

'I hear you and Mrs Sloane are gonna be headin' off to San Antonio,' remarked Johnson as he helped Harrison store the stolen money in the supply wagon.

'That's right, I might decide to settle down there.'

'You can get the stage to San Antonio if you want to. It stops at Benficklin on the return journey from El Paso.'

'Benficklin, where's that?'

'It's five miles from Fort Concho, across the river from San Angela. Folks in San Angela ain't too pleased now Benficklin's the county seat but it makes sense. There's a spring, a post office and the headquarters of the stage company runnin' the mail route there.'

'I might just do that. I'm getting tired of sitting on a horse all day.'

'Well, just another two days of it to go. Then you can get on that coach and forget all your troubles.'

Maggie smiled knowingly when Harrison told her of his plan. 'I already thought the same thing. By all accounts Benficklin's a more respectable place than San Angela anyway, a much nicer place to stay while we wait for the stage.'

'You seem to have it all worked out.'

'Of course I do, John. I'm a woman, aren't I? Besides, we're safe now; what else can go wrong?'

Harrison wondered about that. They were still a long way from Fort Concho.

10

Bleary-eyed, they set off again at dawn. As the morning passed the light breeze that had been stirring grew stronger until it was a wind that whistled through the canvas awning of the supply wagon and blew sand up into their faces. Johnson pointed to a cloud against the horizon, no bigger than a man's hand.

'There's a sandstorm comin' and we're headed right into it.'

Harrison looked around him, but there was no sign of anywhere they might shelter. 'We don't appear to have much choice.'

'You're right, ain't no canyon for miles around.'

Harrison urged Maggie to seek shelter from the wind. She sighed, then muttered something about not being made of china but reluctantly agreed to ride in the wagon for a time. As she settled down among the sacks and barrels he assured her that it would not be for long, then he rejoined the column beside Johnson. The wind seemed to blow more strongly with every step and as the sand was whipped up it became increasingly difficult to see. They tied handkerchiefs around their mouths and bound their hats on to their heads with scarves as they inched forward. They gave up trying to speak to one another as their muffled voices were lost in the howling gale, but still they trudged on.

Eventually Kinsella held up his sword to call a halt. The message was passed down the line as most of them could no longer see the front of the column. Further gestures indicated that they were to move the four wagons round in a circle and shelter inside it as best they could, it being impossible to continue any further. While this was being done a wheel splintered and came off the main supply wagon so that it lurched dangerously and almost fell sideways on to the ground. Maggie stumbled out of the back and Harrison hurried over to her, but she indicated that she was unhurt.

Men and their horses huddled inside the ring of wagons for over an hour while the sandstorm raged about them. The shelter was woefully inadequate and a sigh of relief swept through the column when the wind eventually died down. As they coughed and sneezed, dusting themselves down as best they could, it was time to survey the damage. The wheel was broken and the axle also appeared to have been damaged. Kinsella stroked his beard.

'We can't fit all our supplies on three wagons so we'll have to fix it somehow.'

'We've got a spare wheel, sir,' Johnson told him.

Kinsella prodded the broken axle with his boot. 'Then we just need to put this right.'

Their conversation was interrupted by the sound of horsemen approaching.

They turned to see a man driving a covered wagon with a passenger beside him and four others on horseback. As they got nearer, it became clear that they were soldiers, flashes of blue were visible beneath the dust on their uniforms. Harrison held up his hand as a signal to stop and they drew up alongside the wagon.

The driver glanced at the damage as he saluted smartly. 'Sergeant Murray, sir, Eighth Cavalry. Looks like you could do with some help.'

Kinsella returned his salute and introduced himself. 'That's right, Sergeant. Do you know how to fix it?'

Murray jumped down. Harrison noticed that he was a wiry man with hard, narrow grey eyes above a blond beard. 'My uncle used to make wagons like these, sir. I partly learned the trade before I was in the army.' He nodded as he examined the damage more closely while Johnson went to fetch the spare wheel.

Murray turned back to his men.

'Macpherson, Fisher, get over here.' Two of the horsemen exchanged looks as they dismounted slowly and came over to help. Directing them to lift the wagon slightly, he felt the damaged area and called to another of his companions. 'Siegel, get me that piece of wood and the tools out of the back.' The man appeared hesitant.

'C'mon, the sooner we get this done for the captain the quicker we can get going,' Murray told him impatiently. Siegel obeyed and soon the sergeant had fixed the axle and was putting the new wheel in place. As he did so the wagon shifted somewhat and a bag tumbled out of the back. There was a moment of silence as it spilled open and some wads of cash fell out on to the ground. One of the men quickly stuffed them back into the bag before putting it away again. Murray said nothing but there was a hunger in his eyes that Kinsella could not fail to notice, and his men looked at the soldiers surrounding them as if weighing up the odds.

'With your permission, sir, we'll be on our way,' said Murray as he straightened up.

Kinsella looked at him coolly. 'Where is that exactly?'

Murray appeared flustered. 'I don't know what you mean, sir.'

'I want to know where you're going, damn it!' growled the officer. 'There are six men out here on their own, some of whom appear rather reluctant to obey your orders. Where are the rest of your troop and your commanding officer?'

Murray quickly recovered himself. 'We're from Fort Worth, sir. Our lieutenant and more than half the troop were killed by the Comanches. Then we got separated from the others in the sandstorm and now we can't find them.'

Kinsella turned to Johnson. 'Take Mr Harrison and see if you can find any trace of Sergeant Murray's companions within a five-mile radius of here. Mrs Sloane may accompany you too, since I understand she has some scouting ability. Look for signs of any Comanches having been in the area.'

'We'll be much obliged, sir, if you can find them,' said Murray as he swallowed hard.

'You'd better hope so because if they aren't found you'll all be arrested for desertion.'

Harrison, Johnson and Maggie could hear the sergeant protesting his innocence as they set off to search the surrounding area. They looked intensively but saw no signs of any battle or other soldiers.

'If there'd been fighting near here you'd expect to see some signs of it, but there's nothing,' said Harrison as his eyes scanned the horizon.

Johnson nodded. 'Yeah, those fellas might be from Fort Worth but I bet they ain't supposed to be out here. They're probably deserters, or maybe outlaws in disguise.'

'I wonder what they're after?' mused Maggie.

Johnson shrugged. 'There's dollars in plenty o' places if you know where to look. Maybe they had a stage robbery planned, or were gonna hit a town that has a bank.'

'In that case it's lucky they've been caught.' Harrison took a final look around. 'Do you think we've seen enough?'

'Yeah, I reckon so.' The sergeant patted his horse as its ears twitched. 'C'mon, let's head back.'

At that moment the sound of distant but rapid gunfire echoed across the desert. All three looked at one another in alarm, and then galloped back towards the column. As they approached it was clear that a massacre had taken place. The ground was littered with dead and dying soldiers, most of whom had suffered numerous gunshot wounds. The mingled smells of blood and gunsmoke hung in the air while, in the distance, a wagon sped away, leaving clouds of dust in its wake. They dismounted quickly, moving among the victims to see if there were any who were not beyond help. Two of Murray's men were among the dead.

Johnson found a young trooper calling out for water and went quickly to his aid. He breathed in short gasps, his chest was riddled with bullet wounds and Harrison realized that there was little they could do for him. He bent down and gently asked him what had happened.

'Murray . . . said he had papers . . . the wagon . . . ' He coughed and blood ran from a corner of his mouth.

'It's all right, son, take it easy,' Harrison told him. Johnson gave him another sip of water and he whispered 'They had . . . a . . . Gatling gun,' before his last breath came with a sigh.

Johnson gently shut the soldier's eyes. 'This poor boy can't have been more than nineteen or twenty.' He stood up. 'At least we know what happened.'

'It sounds like Murray claimed he had papers in his wagon which proved his story. Captain Kinsella told him to fetch them which gave Murray and his men the chance to open fire on the entire column.'

Johnson nodded. 'Yeah. Those damn things fire two hundred rounds a minute so our boys never stood a chance, and neither will we if we go after 'em.'

'I wouldn't be so sure about that, Sergeant.'

They all turned in amazement to see Kinsella staggering towards them, blood running from a wound across his forehead. The two rushed forward to steady him as Maggie attempted to stanch the flow of blood.

'It looks worse than it is,' he assured them. 'A bullet glanced across my forehead when they first attacked. I was knocked out and fell to the ground.' The captain looked around with horror at the carnage which surrounded them. 'My God, they'll pay for this, I swear it. Get me a horse.'

Harrison shook his head. 'You're in no fit state to ride. Besides, what can the four of us do against a Gatling gun?'

'I can ride well enough but you're right about that gun. They'd just pick us off.'

'Why don't we just follow their trail but keep out of firing range? At least that way we'll know where they've gone,' suggested Maggie.

'Be headin' for the border if they've any sense.' Johnson bent down and drew in the dirt with a stick. 'The quickest way from here is towards Fort Concho, where we're goin'. I reckon they'll stop over in San Angela and then head towards Del Rio.' He made a mark on the ground at the edge of his crude map and they all looked at it.

Harrison thought for a moment. 'It will take them a few days. My guess is that they'll hide out in San Angela to rest and they'll probably ditch those uniforms.'

'Then what are we waiting for?' asked Kinsella. 'Once we get there we'll search the town until we find them. We can get more men from Fort Concho if necessary.' He turned and peered into the back of the supply wagon which had contained the money. 'The cash has all gone, of course. I suspect greed

176

drove them as much as their desire to escape.'

The horses which escaped injury had fled when their riders were shot, frightened by the rapidity of the gunfire but one now came trotting back, sniffing among the corpses for its rider. Kinsella seized the creature's bridle and swung himself into the saddle. Once again, he was in command, possessed of a steely resolve to catch those who had murdered his men. They set off then at a steady pace, slowing when they spotted a wagon and two horsemen in the distance. Kinsella peered through a telescope at his quarry. 'At least there are only four of them now which will even up the odds if we have the element of surprise.'

'It will do as long as they don't spot that they're being followed,' Harrison remarked.

'That's a good point so we'll stop for the night soon, before they do. After all, we know where they are going.'

They passed an uneventful night but

Harrison slept badly. The massacre of the troops played on his mind and he saw images of their dead faces when he closed his eyes. The loss of the money did not concern him particularly, but he was determined that those who had butchered Kinsella's men would not profit from their actions. The morning brought relief from his nightmares but the face that stared back from his shaving mirror appeared drawn and tired. Kinsella approached him as he scraped the last of the soap from his chin.

'Murray and his gang will probably have set off by now. We'd best get moving.'

Harrison had not heard his words for, reflected in the shaving mirror, he had seen Swift Eagle and his band advancing on their camp. They were moving slowly and no war cry was uttered but their movements were purposeful. He turned to look at them and Kinsella followed his gaze with a gasp of horror.

'God damn it, we stand no chance out here! I told you they couldn't be trusted!'

Harrison remained calm. 'We don't know what they want yet.'

Johnson was now standing behind them. 'He's right, sir. If they were gonna attack I figure they wouldn't lose any time doin' it.'

At last the Comanches halted just a few yards from them. Swift Eagle spoke first. 'My scouts saw many soldiers die from the great gun your enemies had.'

'So, have you come to finish us off?' Kinsella asked him.

The chief looked indignant. 'Your question is foolish, Fire-face. I know you were returning to your fort. My people will keep the peace we have made.'

'Then what do you want?' Kinsella's tone was now somewhat less hostile.

'My scouts still follow these enemies of yours who laugh as the hyena laughs over the bodies of your men. I come to ask if you wish us to kill them or bring them to you alive?'

Kinsella was nonplussed. 'I don't understand. Why would you do that?'

'You have made peace with us so we will help you. We do not fear their great gun.'

'Their bullets can kill your braves as easily as they killed my men,' Kinsella told him.

Swift Eagle smiled. 'They saw my scouts but their gun would not speak fire, it was silent. The Great Spirit protects us.'

'Those Gatling guns jam easily, sir. I reckon Murray won't be able to fix it,' Johnson whispered to him.

Kinsella nodded. 'Why don't we all ride together, Swift Eagle? We'll catch up with these men while they're out in the open. I'd like them taken alive if possible.'

The chief nodded his assent, then spoke to his followers in Comanche to explain what had been decided. Within minutes they were on their way, riding hard to close the gap between themselves and their quarry. It was a strange turn of events, Harrison thought, that brought Kinsella and his arch enemy together in an alliance like this, since the captain was a renowned 'Indian fighter': one of those who believed that the Indian tribes had to be subjugated and integrated into American society as peaceful farmers and tradesmen. Nevertheless, Harrison could tell that he was a decent man at heart.

These thoughts were interrupted by the sight of a wagon and two horsemen in the distance. As they came within range there were rifle shots from two men who were riding in the back. It was clear that the Gatling gun had jammed and was not working, but they were good marksmen nonetheless. One of the Comanches tumbled from his horse as he was hit, quickly followed by another. Swift Eagle raised the spear he was carrying, which was a signal for his men to divide into two columns and attack the wagon from each side. Harrison veered to the right behind Kinsella and soon drew level with one of the horsemen, who fired at him and narrowly missed. Harrison held the reins firmly in his right hand and shot with his left, hitting his opponent squarely in the chest. The man's arms flew up and he fell back from his horse. The fugitives were not ready to give up, though, and the wagon increased in speed to pull away as Murray desperately lashed the horses.

The men in the back were still firing and had killed several Comanches but two warriors now clambered on to the roof of the wagon, sliced through the canvas awning and jumped inside to overpower them. The other horseman was hit in the throat by an arrow and fell sideways from his saddle. Kinsella drew level with Murray and the man who sat beside him on the wagon, a burly individual who also appeared to be a good shot with a rifle. The two warriors who had climbed on to the wagon were now about to attack him from behind but he turned with one swift movement and shot them both. It was just long enough for Kinsella to take aim and fire with his revolver. The bullet caught the man in the neck and he slumped sideways with a surprised look on his face.

Now only Murray remained as two Comanches mounted the leading horses and cut the harnesses. The wagon rolled on for a few yards before it turned over and he leaped clear, rolling over as he hit the ground. They all drew to a halt in a big circle to surround him. Murray staggered to his feet, gun in hand and looked around desperately for an escape route.

Kinsella moved towards him. 'I want you alive, Murray, so you can face a court martial and then a firing squad. Drop that gun or I'll hand you over to the Comanches.'

There was a moment of hesitation before Murray made up his mind. Then he tossed the revolver down on to the ground.

'Tie him on to a horse, Sergeant,' said Kinsella as he looked with unconcealed contempt at the man kneeling in front of him.

While Johnson busied himself with their prisoner Harrison searched the wagon and found the missing money. 'It's all here,' he said, and he tossed the bags out one by one. Meanwhile the Comanches helped themselves to souvenirs from the battle, taking tunics and hats from the bodies of the deserters. Then it was time to go their separate ways.

Swift Eagle spoke first. 'We leave now, Fire-face.'

Kinsella raised a hand in farewell. 'I'm sure we'll meet again.'

'Will it be to fight or make more of your treaties?' the chief asked, but then he left without waiting for a reply.

'You were right about one thing, Mr Harrison,' murmured Kinsella as he watched them go. 'The Comanche keep their word. They didn't attack us because you got them to agree not to. That's more than can be said for our politicians, who don't stick to the agreements

they make with these people. I'm beginning to realize that's half the trouble,
and coming down hard on them won't
solve it.'

Harrison smiled. It was the nearest
thing to an apology he was going to get.

11

They salvaged what supplies they needed from the broken wagon, using two of the horses as pack animals. Murray's hands were bound to the saddle of the horse he rode, which Johnson tethered to his own mount. Maggie and Harrison each took charge of a pack-horse while Kinsella led the way in front.

'How much further is it to Fort Concho?' asked Maggie as they set off once more.

'We lost our way a bit in that sand-storm. By my reckoning we should arrive tomorrow at about noon,' Kinsella told her.

She shuddered then and stole a glance at their prisoner.

Murray noticed and grinned, despite his predicament. 'Don't you worry about me, my pretty one. I'll treat you real nice if you just untie my hands.'

'Just you shut that mouth o' yours or I swear I'll put an end to your miserable life right here and now,' Johnson warned him.

'Take it easy, Sergeant,' Kinsella said gently. 'This man is our prisoner. He surrendered and we have a duty to deliver him to the proper authorities. He's only to be shot if he attacks us or tries to escape.'

'Lucky for you Captain Kinsella here's a gentleman, but if you wanna try anythin', go right ahead. I'll be ready.' Johnson held up his revolver to show that he meant business.

Murray did not respond but his narrow eyes flitted from one to the other, as if weighing them all up. Harrison sensed that the man was waiting for an opportunity to start something and resolved to keep a close eye on him until they reached their destination. After all, the renegade sergeant was virtually a condemned man and as such he had nothing to lose. The landscape was changing as they drew nearer to the mouth of the

River Concho. It was less arid now with more trees and shrubs and a few wooded slopes. Kinsella held up his hand to draw them to a halt as they arrived at a creek.

'None of us ate this morning. We'll stop here and rest awhile.'

Harrison lit a fire, made coffee and cooked some beans while Maggie tended to the horses. Johnson untied Murray's hands to allow him to dismount, then stood well back, covering him with a revolver as their prisoner climbed from his horse. 'Now, turn around, put your hands behind your head and kneel down.'

There was a brief hesitation on Murray's part before the sergeant gestured with his weapon. 'C'mon man, just do it.'

Harrison left his cooking and came over to help Johnson by covering him with his gun. The sergeant then approached their prisoner and tied his hands tightly behind his back. Then he pushed him face down in the dirt and bound his feet with the other end of the rope.

'God damn it, how am I supposed to eat like this?' demanded Murray sourly as he struggled to get into a sitting position against a nearby boulder. There was just enough slack in the rope to allow him this much movement, but no more.

'Nobody said you was gonna eat. A man on an empty stomach ain't got no energy to fight so I figure you can wait until we get you locked up safe and sound,' Johnson told him.

'We can't let a man starve, no matter what he's done,' remarked Maggie as she brought over a plate of beans. Then, kneeling in front of him, she fed Murray with a spoon. The sergeant shook his head but said nothing, while their captive tried to engage his benefactor in conversation.

'Where are you from, lady?' he asked her.

'Don't talk, just eat,' she told him, her tone cold.

'Aw, c'mon now. Can't you just be a little friendly?'

Harrison cut in. 'That's enough. You can see the lady doesn't want to talk to you so just be quiet.'

'Are you her pa or somethin'?' sneered Murray.

Harrison went and stood over him. 'It's still a long way to Fort Concho. I suggest you don't try our patience too much.'

Maggie shovelled the last of the beans into his mouth as Murray wordlessly eyed the pearl-handled revolvers Harrison had in each holster. Then, after a brief rest, they were ready to get going again. Johnson cut the rope binding Murray's feet and led him over to his horse. Once he had hauled himself back into the saddle at gunpoint he was tied to the animal and ready to be led away. Then a folded sheet of paper fell out from inside Murray's tunic. Johnson picked it up. He gasped as he read its contents.

'Hey, listen up! It says here that Dan Murray is wanted for tryin' to rob a bank in Colorado and killin' three folks, one of 'em a little girl!' He looked up at their captive.

'I didn't mean to kill that kid, it was an accident,' muttered Murray in response.

Harrison and Kinsella came over to look at the poster. 'It doesn't say anything about you being in the army,' the officer remarked.

Murray shrugged. 'We figured army uniforms were a good disguise. So what?'

Kinsella looked at him with distaste. 'It means we'll have to hand you over to the civilian authorities, especially in view of this other crime. You'll still be charged with murdering my men but if a US marshal turns up with a warrant, you could be sent to Colorado to hang.'

'I guess we'll have to take him to the county jail in Benficklin,' said Harrison.

Murray grinned. 'That's just fine by me. I've busted outta jails before.'

They all ignored him, their horses splashing across the creek as they continued on their way.

'There sure is a lotta money in those bags,' remarked Murray as Harrison rode past him. The outlaw then spoke more quietly as he leaned towards him. 'I could use some help from a man who's handy with a gun.'

Harrison shook his head. 'The only help you'll get is up the steps to the gallows.'

'What's wrong with you? You're a civilian, same as me, so why should you care about some dumb payroll? If we take care o' these folks it's a straight split down the middle.'

'You're wrong, Murray. I may not be a soldier but I'm nothing like you and I never will be.'

As Harrison rode on Johnson asked, 'What did he want with you?'

'What everyone wants: that damned money.'

Johnson patted his holster. 'If he makes a move I'll be ready.'

Behind them Murray rubbed the knot on the rope binding his hands against the pommel of his saddle. He had managed to loosen it slightly but not nearly enough. It was a pity that Harrison was too foolish to take advantage of a good opportunity when it presented itself, but he still hoped for a chance to get away before they reached Benficklin.

They rode on through the heat of the day until Kinsella called them to a halt once more and suggested that they rest for an hour to rest the horses.

Maggie shuddered as Harrison sat down beside her. 'That Murray makes my skin crawl. I wish we didn't have to drag him along with us.'

He put an arm around her shoulders. 'It's not for long, we'll be there tomorrow. Then we can hand the money over and get Murray safely locked up.'

The subject of their conversation was watching them with interest. If the opportunity arose, the woman would make a suitable hostage. The knife Murray always kept inside his left boot was still there but so far there had been no way of getting to it without being shot. He would have to bide his time, time that was running out with every mile they rode.

Johnson prodded their prisoner with his boot. 'Time to get movin', so c'mon.'

At that moment, Kinsella approached them. 'It's all right, Sergeant, I'll guard him for a while. You know this terrain pretty well so why don't you ride up in front?'

Johnson beamed back at him. 'Thank you very much, sir. I don't mind if I do.'

Murray scowled as Kinsella adjusted his bonds but then an idea occurred to him.

'I have to answer a call o' nature, sir. I could use that clump o' trees over there.'

'Oh, all right man, but hurry up about it,' said Kinsella as he hauled him to his feet.

They reached the trees and Murray adjusted his clothing. Kinsella stood close, his gun at the other man's ribs.

'I can't do it with you watchin' me like that,' grumbled the outlaw. Kinsella sighed but turned aside slightly which just allowed his prisoner time to bend down and retrieve his knife. He moved swiftly and the blade plunged into the officer's heart, while his killer caught the gun as it fell from Kinsella's numbed fingers. He dragged the body further into the trees and then peered through the foliage. They were all busy with their horses but Maggie was standing on the edge of the group, slightly nearer to him. He moved swiftly, wasting no time.

Maggie was just tightening the girth strap on her horse when a knife was pressed against her throat. Murray's right arm was around her waist and she could see that he was holding a gun.

'Don't scream,' he whispered. 'Just do like I say and you won't get hurt.' He moved her around so that he was now standing nearer to her horse, with her body shielding his.

'Look what I've got!' he called to the

others. They both turned to face him and he grinned at their horrified expressions. 'Take off your gunbelts and toss 'em towards me.'

'Where's Captain Kinsella?' demanded Johnson.

'He's dead, so do as I say or she'll get the same. Remember, I've got nothin' to lose.'

'We'd better go along with him for now,' whispered Harrison as he slowly unbuckled his gunbelt and threw it across. Johnson did the same with an obvious show of reluctance and their weapons landed just a few feet away from Murray.

With his left hand he still held a knife at Maggie's throat while pointing a gun at them with his right. 'Now, get down on your knees and put your hands behind your heads.'

'You won't get far, I promise you that,' said Harrison as he knelt down.

'Well, you sure as hell won't be followin' me,' jeered his adversary. Then, flinging his captive to one side, he stepped forward and cocked his gun. 'So long, fellas,' he said as he took aim.

Maggie felt the rock in her hand as she stumbled to her feet. Murray did not hear her behind him as he began to squeeze the trigger and his shot misfired harmlessly as a solid lump of sandstone crashed into the back of his head. He stumbled forward with a groan before falling to his knees. In vain he tried to raise himself and aim his weapon once more, then he keeled over on to his side and lay still.

'Is he dead?' Maggie asked as Harrison removed the gun from Murray's inert fingers.

'No, you just knocked him out. He'll wake up in a few hours with an almighty headache.' He looked up at her. 'You saved our lives just now. Thanks.'

'Yeah,' added Johnson, 'I thought our time was up for sure.' He picked up the unconscious Murray and flung him across his shoulders before putting him across a horse with feet and hands bound securely to the stirrups.

They buried Kinsella in a shallow grave while Maggie read the Twenty-Third Psalm. Their journey continued in silence, the officer's death having cast a pall of gloom over their journey. It grew dark after two hours and they stopped for the night. Harrison pulled Murray down from his horse and bound him securely to a nearby tree. 'You make one move tonight and you're dead, understand?' he told him firmly.

The outlaw nodded in reply. He knew there was no chance of escape now and he still felt weak after being hit over the head with that rock. This time he said nothing when Maggie fed him and wisely drifted off to sleep rather than taunting his captors as he usually did.

'It looks like Murray's got the message,' remarked Johnson as he finished his beans.

They took turns guarding him nonetheless. A man desperate to cheat the noose could be capable of anything, as the outlaw had already proved. Harrison had the last watch and sat contentedly as an orange sunrise filtered through the morning mist. Today they would at last reach their destination, hand over the stolen money, and he and Maggie could get on with the rest of their lives. These pleasant thoughts were interrupted as Murray awoke and stretched his bound limbs as best he could.

'What are you lookin' so pleased about?' he asked sourly.

'The thought of you at the end of a rope,' replied Harrison cheerfully.

'I wouldn't count on it.'

'Well, you'll be behind bars by this afternoon and if you try anything before then I won't hesitate to shoot. Just remember that.'

The others were stirring now and Harrison went to a nearby stream where he washed himself as best he could. He perched on the bank to shave and then dressed hurriedly.

'How about some breakfast?' Johnson

asked upon his return. 'I'm afraid it's just beans and coffee again, that's all we've left.'

'I don't mind, it's better than having to starve.'

They made sure Murray was bound securely on his horse before they left. The mist soon cleared and it was another hot, bright day in West Texas. They made steady progress throughout the morning and were just a few miles from their destination when Johnson drew to a halt and dismounted.

'What's the matter?' Harrison asked him.

'My horse limps a little. I reckon there's a problem with the shoe on his left foreleg but there's a good black-smith in San Angela. It's best if we stop by there on the way.'

They passed through some farmland before reaching San Angela, a bustling frontier town packed with saloons, gambling dens and hotels which were little more than brothels. The main street was a dirt road, crowded with off-duty soldiers, hucksters, tradesmen and young women in gaudy outfits. No one paid them any attention as they went their way, it being a place where strangers came and went quite frequently. At last they halted outside a forge where a stocky middle-aged man in a leather apron was busily welding the two ends of a broken stirrup back together. Johnson approached him just as he finished the job.

'My horse has a problem with one o' his shoes, mister. It don't seem to fit right.'

'Let me take a look.' The man examined the shoe carefully. 'Yeah, I can fix that.'

As the blacksmith got on with his work a slim, moustachioed figure in a white apron emerged from the saloon across the street and came over towards them.

'Good afternoon, *señora*,' he said to Maggie with a bow 'and to you too, *señores*. I am Victor Esterhaz and I own the saloon across the street.' He gestured towards Murray, still bound to his horse. 'I could not help noticing that you are guarding a prisoner. I wondered whether you would like me to bring you over some beers, on the house of course, as I am so pleased to see criminals being apprehended at last in this lawless place.'

Johnson beamed in response. 'Well that's mighty decent of you.'

Esterhaz bowed again before asking what their prisoner had done, gasping with disapproval as Johnson recounted the outlaw's crimes.

Esterhaz shook his head and looked at Murray with disgust before hastily crossing himself. 'I have never heard such a tale of evil. You'd better start praying for your soul; no beer for you!' Then he turned to Maggie. 'And for you, *señora*?'

'A glass of cold water will be just fine, thank you.'

Esterhaz bowed again and hurried back across the street to his saloon. Harrison wondered why the Mexican was so friendly and interested in what they were doing. No doubt they would find out soon enough.

★ ★ ★

Jorge and Pablo were still at the bar when Esterhaz returned with his information. 'The one tied up tried to steal the money. The other soldiers are dead, apart from Johnson.'

'Where's the money now?' asked Jorge.

'They've got some bags on those packhorses, so it's probably in those.'

Pablo gazed longingly through the window. 'It's so near; if only we could just take it.'

Esterhaz shook his head. 'What? Start a gunfight in broad daylight out there in the street? We'd have soldiers from the fort down on us in no time. No, I'll take these drinks across and see what else I can find out.'

They drained their beers quickly but Esterhaz stayed to engage them in conversation.

203

'What are you going to do with him?' he asked Johnson, looking at their prisoner.

'Murray's goin' to the county jail in Benficklin. He's a civilian and wanted for other crimes, so I guess it'll be up to a judge to decide whether the army deals with him or not.'

By now the blacksmith had finished his work; Johnson paid him and they were ready to leave. Harrison climbed wearily back on to his horse and Esterhaz approached him, smiling.

'If you need somewhere to stay, señor, I have rooms free for you and the señora.'

'Thank you, but we already have rooms in Benficklin.'

'Why did you tell him we already had rooms,' Maggie asked as they rode away.

'I don't know. There was just something about him I can't quite trust. He had that hungry look in his eyes, a look I've seen too many times on this trip.'

Maggie shuddered. 'I hope you're just imagining things. I thought once we got this far we could leave all that behind us.'

Johnson led them through the town in a westerly direction, past a bakery, a carriage shop and a saloon called The Grey Mule. He stopped at this point as a soldier was hurled through the swing back doors and lay sprawled in the dirt in front of them. The sergeant shook his head as he skilfully guided his horse around the prone figure.

'That there soldier's known as Dead Ellis cos once he drank so much we all thought he was dead. We put him in the hospital and laid him out in a coffin and suddenly he started twitchin'. We been callin' him Dead Ellis ever since. The man got a terrible fright but he ain't never gonna quit drinkin'.'

They turned then on to Chadbourne Street, past a livery stables and up a hill where they could see Fort Concho and the river below them. They rode down the other side, through grasses that reached up to their stirrups, turned alongside the river and through the entrance past rows of limestone buildings with pecan wood rafters. The fort was a hive of activity and Johnson pointed out the barracks for enlisted men, a commissary, hospital and chapel. He called over the sentry as they reached the officers' quarters and they were quickly shown into Colonel Grierson's office, with a military escort to guard Murray and carry the money.

Grierson was in his late forties and his most prominent feature was a dark, luxuriant beard, lightly speckled with grey. He wore his hair long and swept forward in a wave across his forehead, looking more like the music teacher he once was than a senior army officer. The colonel rose from behind a desk littered with papers as they entered and acknowledged Johnson's salute before turning to the others.

'You must be Mr Harrison. I heard about your exploits at Jacob's Well, and we're indebted to you, sir.' His handshake was warm but with strength and determination in its grip. Harrison introduced Maggie and Grierson bowed slightly. Then he looked at the bound figure of Murray and frowned. Johnson handed Grierson the wanted poster and he studied it carefully. As he did so the sergeant told him briefly what had become of Kinsella and the rest of the troop. The colonel paled visibly and dropped back into his chair. He covered his face while he composed himself, then he looked up again at Murray.

'You'll stay in the county jail until it's decided whether you hang for the death of that little girl or the soldiers you've killed.' Then he held up a wad of bank-notes from one of the bags. 'Take a good look, Murray, because it's the last you'll see of it. I'm sending this money by the next stage to our depot in San Antonio. Think about that when they put the rope around your neck.' Then he signalled to the guards to take the outlaw away.

After Murray was led out Johnson

gave the colonel a fuller account of their adventures. Grierson listened intently, occasionally asking brief questions.

'That's quite a story,' he said when Johnson had finished. 'However, it's not quite over yet. As I said, I have orders to send that money on to San Antonio, but can't spare the men for a payroll wagon so I'm sending it by stage instead. A lot of money is sent by mail coach these days but I'd feel more comfortable if you and Sergeant Johnson went with it.'

'As a matter of fact I'm going to San Antonio anyway,' Harrison told him.

'Good, that's settled. You'll have earned your share of the ten per cent of the payroll I've been authorized to pay as a reward. It will be divided equally between the three of you.'

Johnson shook his head. 'There ain't no call for that. I was just doing my job.'

'I think you went beyond your duty, Johnson,' Grierson told him. 'I'm awarding you a commendation as well.'

'Thank you, sir,' he replied, visibly moved by the gesture.

The colonel turned back to Harrison. 'The stagecoach leaves the day after tomorrow outside the post office. Sergeant Johnson will meet you there with the money in a strongbox.'

Grierson showed them out then and a groom led their horses over as they left the officers' quarters. Johnson gave them directions to Benficklin, which was about three miles away on the other side of the river and soon Harrison and Maggie were on their way.

12

Murray lay on the hard, narrow bed in his cell, dreaming of escape. He was surprised to see Esterhaz walk in and greet Joe Samuels, the deputy guarding him.

'Hello there, Victor. What brings you here?' replied Samuels, who sometimes frequented the saloons in San Angela and knew Esterhaz well.

'I brought some food for your prisoner.' Esterhaz unwrapped the cloth bundle he was carrying to reveal a steak sandwich and a bottle of beer. 'I think I know him from some place so is it OK if I talk to him for a while?'

Samuels shrugged. 'I guess so, he ain't goin' nowhere until Judge Hawkins gets here.'

Esterhaz winked conspiratorially at the prisoner as he drew up a stool and passed the bottle and the food through the bars. Murray took a swig and then a large bite from the sandwich.

'So, *amigo*, where do I know you from?' began Esterhaz.

'Del Rio maybe?' suggested the prisoner, his mouth full.

'Yes, I had a little cantina there before I came out this way. You came in regularly.'

Murray nodded enthusiastically, joining in the charade. 'Yeah, I thought I recognized you when you came in. Good old Victor, fancy you rememberin' Dan Murray!'

Esterhaz smiled and glanced surreptitiously behind him to see if Samuels was paying attention to their conversation but the man was engrossed in cleaning his gun.

'I'm sorry to see you here, Dan. I always told you no good would come of stealing from honest folk.' Esterhaz wagged an admonishing finger, winking once more as he added 'So, do you know what's happened to that payroll you almost got away with?'

'It's up at the fort.' Murray felt his heartbeat quicken as he realized the reason for his visitor's pretence of knowing him. If a robbery was planned, perhaps they would need him.

'The money won't be there for long though,' he added with a thin-lipped smile. 'I heard Colonel Grierson say he was sendin' it on the next stage to the army depot in San Antonio. Them fellas you was talkin' to this afternoon will be guardin' it.'

'A trip to San Antonio would be nice, wouldn't it?' Esterhaz grinned and gave another wink as he said this.

'It sure would. If I weren't stuck in here I'd like that,' replied Murray with a nod.

The Mexican rose from his stool with a sigh. 'You've only yourself to blame, I'm afraid, but I'll pray for your soul, *amigo*.'

As Esterhaz left he turned to Samuels and said, 'I tell you what. Why don't I bring over some of my best whiskey and a couple of friends to keep you company tomorrow night?'

Samuels shook his head reluctantly. 'That's real good of you, Victor but I'm not supposed to do that when I'm guarding a prisoner.'

'What harm can it do? He's safely locked up and you've got the key. Besides, a couple of drinks won't stop you shooting him if he tries to escape.'

'I guess not. Just don't let anyone see you, that's all.'

Esterhaz tapped the side of his nose with his finger. 'Of course not. *Adios amigos.*'

★　★　★

Jorge and Pablo could hardly believe their good fortune when Esterhaz told them what he had learned. With Murray out of jail there would be four of them to carry out the robbery and share the loot. By choosing the right spot to launch an attack and using the element of surprise, they might just get away with it.

'There'll be a posse out after Murray,' Jorge reminded them. 'What about that?'

'We'll get him out the night before the stage leaves and his escape won't be discovered until the morning. The posse will head for the border because that's what they'll expect Murray to do.' Esterhaz drained the last of his tequila. 'Meanwhile, we'll rob the stage and then split.'

'You're a genius!' said Pablo. 'We'll be long gone before the gringos learn the truth.'

They spoke in low voices and paid no attention to the hopeless drunk at the end of the bar but Dead Ellis had very acute hearing and a habit of eavesdropping. He drained the last of his beer, rose unsteadily to his feet and headed back to the fort. He had not gone far when he ran into Johnson, who was enjoying an evening off duty.

'Mexicans! Gonna r-r-rob the ssshtage!' babbled Ellis, grabbing the sergeant's tunic.

Johnson drew back from the stench of whiskey as he held the man upright. 'What are you talkin' about?' he demanded. 'If it wasn't for me bein' off duty you'd be on a charge!'

Ellis grew more insistent. 'They're gonna get M-M-M-urray outta jail . . . I shwear it!'

Johnson frowned. This was starting to make sense and was clearly far more than the confused ramblings of a drunk. 'Where did you hear this?' he asked. Ellis pointed back towards the saloon he had just come from. The sergeant followed as his companion stumbled ahead of him and then gestured for him to look through a window to the left of the swing-back doors.

'I thought we'd seen the last o' them fellas for sure,' whispered Johnson as he spotted Esterhaz talking to Jorge and the fat bandit who had been with Swift Eagle when the Comanches attacked the column.

'You know 'em?' Ellis asked, rapidly sobering up in his excitement.

'Yeah, sure I do. Now I know why Esterhaz was askin' all them questions this afternoon. Did they say when they were gonna get Murray?'

Ellis frowned as he tried to remember. 'Lemme see . . . night 'fore the stage leaves.'

'That's tomorrow night. You'd better get back to the fort while I go find Mr Harrison in Benficklin. We'll report this to Colonel Grierson in the morning when you've sobered up.'

Ellis nodded reluctantly and set off home while Johnson went to the livery stables to fetch his horse. He needed to find which hotel Harrison was in and quickly.

*   *   *

Harrison eased his aching limbs out of the hot tub and towelled himself dry. The freshly laundered shirt felt soft against his skin and he enjoyed getting dressed in clean clothes after so many days on the road. He had barely

216

finished when heard a knock on the door and opened it, to find Johnson on the threshold, twisting his hat in his hands as a frown contorted his features.

'I'm sorry to disturb you, John, but we got a problem.'

He gestured towards a chair by the window and the sergeant dropped into it before telling him about what he and Dead Ellis had seen through the window of the saloon.

Harrison paced the room as he listened intently. 'We could let them go ahead with their plan but ask for an armed escort for the stage,' he suggested.

'They might call it off and then they'd just get away, Murray as well. Even if they didn't, there's a lotta them narrow canyons where they could ambush us.'

'Yes, you're right. They have to be stopped before the robbery but the trouble is, this is all hearsay. There's nothing that would stand up in any court.'

'I guess they'll have to get caught

springin' Murray from jail then,' said Johnson.

'That's just what I was thinking, Eli, but the people of Benficklin won't like having a shootout in the centre of their town. Someone might get hurt.'

Johnson stood up and put his hat back on. 'Well, I'd best be gettin' back. We can see Colonel Grierson about this first thing tomorrow. He'll know what to do for the best.' Then, as he opened the door he turned and said, 'Are you goin' to tell Mrs Sloane about this?'

Harrison sighed. Yes, he would tell her and no doubt she would insist on going with them to see the colonel tomorrow. He knew her well enough by now to know that.

* * *

Colonel Grierson looked at the four people assembled in his office. He had listened carefully to what he was told and was convinced that the threat was real. Why else would two of Harrison's enemies have turned up in San Angela? He stuffed some tobacco into his pipe and lit it as he considered what to do.

'You're right about none of this standing up in court,' he told Harrison as he exhaled a cloud of blue smoke. 'This is one of the rare occasions on which Ellis here appears to be completely sober, but the state he was in last night could result in his testimony being dismissed.'

Ellis shifted uncomfortably. 'I know what I heard, sir.'

Grierson nodded. 'We all believe you but that's not the point.' The colonel leaned back in his chair. 'We can't risk them attacking the stage, as you've pointed out, so that means doing something when they try to free Murray.'

'We could either storm the jail or wait until they've got Murray out and are leaving,' suggested Harrison.

Grierson drew on his pipe. 'I favour a more subtle solution, Mr Harrison; one in which our quarry can be trapped inside the jail.'

'Will it be dangerous?' asked Maggie.

'It will be less dangerous to the people of Benficklin than a gun battle in the middle of their town, but perhaps more dangerous for those involved.'

'Go on, Colonel.' Harrison was intrigued.

As Grierson unfolded his plan, they were all impressed by its audacity and ingenuity while also appreciating the risk it posed to their own lives. 'I must emphasize that I am not giving any orders here. If anyone feels unable to take part, there will be no shame in it,' the colonel concluded. He paused for a moment but no objections were raised.

Harrison felt Maggie squeeze his arm. 'You don't have to do this, John.'

He patted her arm. 'I know but I've come this far and I always see a job through to the end.'

She sighed. 'I just hope you all know what you're doing.'

Grierson puffed on his pipe. 'Have a little faith, Mrs Sloane. If I didn't think this was going to work I wouldn't have suggested it.'

★   ★   ★

It was early evening when a covered wagon drew up at the rear of the jail in Benficklin. Johnson jumped down from the driver's seat and waited until there were no passers-by. He knocked on the side of the wagon and Harrison emerged from the back. The prison clothes were a poor fit and his false beard itched but the disguise would have to do. After all, he would not be seen at close quarters until the final moments. The escort of four soldiers remained in the wagon as the two men hurried inside the jail.

Samuels had received Grierson's note and was expecting them. 'Come on, we'd better hurry it up. Esterhaz and his friends will be here soon.'

Murray got up from his bunk as the cell door was unlocked. Johnson kept him covered with his revolver and gestured for him to come out.

'I ain't goin' no place' said the prisoner sourly.

Johnson drew back the hammer on his gun. 'I figure on usin' this if I must, so move!'

Murray came out and was quickly handcuffed by Samuels while Harrison slipped inside the cell in his place. Moments later Johnson was driving the wagon back to Fort Concho with Murray under guard in the back. Samuels sat down at his desk as if everything was normal while Harrison stretched out on the bunk and turned his face to the wall. The day was drawing to a close and he knew that he would not have long to wait.

Esterhaz, Jorge and Pablo arrived within an hour and two bottles of whiskey were placed on the table as they drew up their chairs. Jorge opened one of the bottles, poured a generous measure into Samuels' glass and a smaller one for each of his companions.

'What about our friend in the cell,

don't he get a drink?' asked Pablo.

Samuels sipped his whiskey. 'He hasn't been feeling too good today and he's asleep now. Let's just leave him, OK?'

Esterhaz shrugged, feigning indifference while hoping that his accomplice would be fit to ride when the time came and, most important, able to do his job the next day.

Samuels was soon winning the poker game, or at least, Esterhaz and his companions were letting him win as they cracked jokes and constantly replenished his glass. Jorge was surprised to see the deputy slurring his words after only a few drinks. This was obviously a man who could not hold his liquor. The three Mexicans exchanged furtive glances. Once Samuels was asleep, it would be time to make their move.

Suddenly there was a loud knocking at the door.

The deputy rose unsteadily from his chair, went to answer it and then was heard to exclaim, 'Why if it ain't my old friend Dead Ellis! C'mon in, fella, we're just playin' a game o' poker.'

'I ain't much good at card games,' said Ellis as he swaggered drunkenly over to the table and dropped into a chair.

Samuels fetched another glass. 'Don't mind about that. Just have a drink with us.' He poured a generous measure out for the soldier and pushed it towards him.

'Are we going to continue playing?' asked Esterhaz nonchalantly. He was unconcerned about the new arrival, considering the drunken soldier no threat to their plans.

'I'll deal,' said Jorge. He gathered the cards together and shuffled them.

'I saw that. You'd better quit dealin' them cards,' said Ellis, eyeing him suspiciously.

'Saw what?' demanded Jorge hotly.

'You feelin' them marks on the backs o' the cards. I know what you're up to.'

'They're Joe's cards and he's been

winning,' Esterhaz told him.

'That don't make no difference. You fellas were just softenin' him up. You must have swapped the cards and now you'll start winnin' instead.'

'That's a lie. Joe, don't listen to him. He's had too much liquor!' protested Jorge.

Suddenly Ellis was on his feet. He swept the cards from the table with a shout of rage. The glasses shook and silver dollars scattered over the floor.

'There's only one way to settle this. Which one of you cheats wants to draw first?'

They were all standing now and it seemed that each man's hand was irresistibly drawn towards his holster. Then Samuels spoke in an effort to restore calm.

'Come on, fellas. This has all been a misunderstanding and we don't want any trouble do we? Why should folks in this town get woken up by people firing guns?' He looked intently at each man and then continued. 'Now you all put your guns outta that window. You can pick 'em up on your way home. I'm the lawman here and what I say goes.'

Esterhaz reluctantly unbuckled his gunbelt. 'You heard what the man said. We don't want any trouble, do we, boys?'

Jorge and Pablo followed suit. They planned to steal the keys from an inebriated Samuels, not shoot anyone, but they disliked giving up their weapons nonetheless.

'What about him?' asked Esterhaz, jerking a thumb at Ellis.

'He's a soldier, so he has to carry his gun all the time, but he won't be firing it, will you, Ellis?'

'No, sir.'

'Good. C'mon fellas, let's get this mess tidied up, start a new game and have a drink.'

They settled down again to play. Ellis sat in surly silence while Samuels appeared to get progressively drunk. Eventually, his head lolled forward and he started to snore.

'I guess I'll be on my way,' said Ellis, rising from the table.

The others waited until he had closed the door behind him, then prepared to make their move. Esterhaz carefully removed the ring of keys from the deputy's belt and went over to unlock the cell. Jorge and Pablo got up from the table and followed.

'Come on, Murray, time to wake up,' hissed Esterhaz through the bars but Harrison lay on his side, his hand on the pearl-handled revolver he had hidden under the pillow. The Mexican stepped inside and put a hand on his shoulder to wake him. Harrison was on his feet in a flash, his gun thrust into a face whose eyes widened in astonishment.

Jorge and Pablo turned to run for the door but a suddenly sober Samuels stopped them in their tracks. 'I think you should stay awhile,' said the deputy. He gestured back towards the cell with his weapon. At that moment Ellis returned, accompanied by Johnson, both men holding their pistols ready.

'You see, boys, I've got plenty of back-up,' said Samuels with a sly smile.

Harrison tossed his false beard to one side without taking his eyes off Esterhaz.

'Drop those keys on the bed and then turn round.'

The Mexican did as he was told and was then ordered to kneel, placing his hands behind his head. Harrison picked up the keys and backed warily out of the cell.

'Go on, get your asses in there too,' said Johnson as he shoved Pablo and Jorge forward. Once they were inside, Harrison locked the door behind them and threw the keys over to Samuels. The three men glowered at them through the bars as Johnson and his companions retreated towards the door.

'Will you be all right, guarding them by yourself?' Harrison asked Samuels.

'Sure I will. You can all get yourselves off to bed now.'

'You haven't seen the last of me,

Harrison. I'll kill you, I swear it!' Jorge called through the bars as they all turned to leave.

'I'll be ready for you,' Harrison replied as he stepped outside.

'I won't lose any sleep about him coming to find me one day; I'll probably be dead by the time he gets out of jail!' Harrison told his companions as they joined him outside. Then Ellis was warmly thanked for his help before he disappeared in search of a drink.

'I'll meet you tomorrow outside the post office,' Johnson reminded Harrison.

Harrison nodded his agreement, then trudged wearily towards his hotel. The long period of waiting in that cell and the constant need to remain alert had tired him more than he realized. He would be glad of a good night's sleep.

Back inside the jail, Jorge pleaded for a drink. 'Give us some of that whiskey, Joe.'

Samuels sighed and took his feet off the table. 'I shouldn't really, so don't tell Sheriff Lawson when he comes in tomorrow, or he'll get mad.'

The deputy poured out three glasses and brought them over. Three sets of hands reached through the bars but it was Jorge who deftly whipped Samuels' gun from its holster. He grinned as his jailer found himself staring helplessly at his own gun.

'The party's over, Joe.' Jorge reached through again to take the keys but Samuels stepped back so that they were out of reach.

'Don't mess with us, just unlock the door or I'll shoot'

There was a split second's hesitation before Samuels decided to make a run for it. It was awkward firing between the bars of a cell door and he calculated that he might just make it. The first shot missed but the second caught him between the shoulders as he reached the table. He pulled it to the ground as he fell, sending its contents rolling across the floor.

The body lay crumpled on the flagstones, the keys out of reach, but

Pablo's long arm stretched out between the bars and managed to grab hold of a foot. Heaving with all his might, he shifted the corpse a fraction nearer the cell. Jorge and Esterhaz could now reach the other foot and with another heave they brought the body near enough to get the keys. Frantically, they unlocked the door and went to pick up their gunbelts.

The two shots, fired one after the other, sounded very loud in the stillness of the night. Harrison spun round, suddenly alert once more. He was sure the noise had come from the jail and ran back towards it, a gun in each hand. Pausing by the window, he peered through in time to see the three prisoners unlock the cell door and pick up their weapons from among the debris on the floor. Pablo was out first and Harrison fired through the window, aiming as best he could. The shot hit Pablo in the face; the burly Mexican threw up his arms with a cry and fell backwards. Jorge and Esterhaz flung themselves down. Harrison could no longer see them from this angle. Cursing, he ran round to the door and kicked it open, then he charged in with both guns blazing.

The next moments passed in a blur. He hit Esterhaz before the lamp was shot out and continued firing into the darkness at the moving shape he sensed just a few feet away. His shots were returned, then there was a sharp pain in his chest before he felt himself falling and his world dissolved into oblivion.

Harrison was running through the desert while ahead of him the wind blew a cloud of hundred-dollar bills. In vain he reached out with his arms to catch them but each time he drew near they were whipped further away from him. He tried to run faster but his legs were as heavy as lead while inside his head a voice echoed, growing ever louder and more insistent: 'It's the Devil's payroll! The Devil's payroll! THE DEVIL'S PAYROLL!!!'

He awoke to feel Maggie wiping his

brow once more with the cool, damp cloth. 'You were having a nightmare, but it's over now.'

Harrison stirred and asked sleepily. 'What the hell happened to me? I feel as if I've been run over by a steam train.'

'You were shot, but a surgeon got the bullet out. and you're going to be fine.'

He frowned as he struggled to remember. 'Did I get the man who did it?'

'You got one of 'em and I got the other,' said Johnson, who had quietly entered the room just in time to witness his friend's recovery.

Harrison smiled weakly. 'Nice work, Eli. What did we do with the money?'

'You don't need to worry about that any more, John. The colonel figured you'd done enough already so he sent it ahead to the army depot by stage with two officers guardin' it.'

'Oh, that's good news.' He looked across to where Maggie was sitting, her eyes glistening with tears. 'Don't cry.

You just said that I'm going to be all right.'

'Yes,' she told him. 'I know you are. From now on we'll both be all right and nothing will ever separate us again.'

'Does that mean you'll marry me?' he whispered.

She nodded her assent. 'I was beginning to think you'd never to ask.'

'I was beginning to think I'd never get the chance.' Then he smiled weakly as he drifted back to sleep, at last finding the peace that had eluded him for so long.

THE END

We do hope that you have enjoyed reading this large print book.

Did you know that all of our titles are available for purchase?

We publish a wide range of high quality large print books including:
Romances, Mysteries, Classics
General Fiction
Non Fiction and Westerns

Special interest titles available in large print are:
The Little Oxford Dictionary
Music Book, Song Book
Hymn Book, Service Book

Also available from us courtesy of Oxford University Press:
Young Readers' Dictionary
(large print edition)
Young Readers' Thesaurus
(large print edition)

For further information or a free brochure, please contact us at:
Ulverscroft Large Print Books Ltd.,
The Green, Bradgate Road, Anstey,
Leicester, LE7 7FU, England.
Tel: (00 44) 0116 236 4325
Fax: (00 44) 0116 234 0205

Other titles in the
Linford Western Library:

HIT 'EM HARD!

Ben Bridges

Arizona Territory, 1882. The Apaches are running rings around the army, raiding, robbing and killing. Captain Nathan Kelso knows they must be confronted on their own terms, hitting fast and hard. But who'd listen to a washed-up, borderline drunk? However, he receives orders to form Company C, a light, mobile unit, dedicated to bracing the Apaches wherever they find them. And after its first mission, deep in Indian country, things just get even tougher for Kelso and Company C.

LET THE GUNS DECIDE

Shane Archer

Death comes to the little town of Macallister in the form of a milk-drinking, baby-faced killer who leaves bodies in the dust. Lone Lee Kirby rides into a town desperate for help, but the body count grows as Kirby is forced to face his own demons.

COLD, HARD CASH

Jake Douglas

It seemed the only way to get out of Red Rock Penitentiary was to die and be shipped out as a corpse. So Dave Jarrett had taken his chance to feign his death and leave Red Rock in a coffin. But enemies, old and new, were all waiting for him to lead them to $70,000. That was when the brutal chain-gang he had left behind began to look far better than dodging bullets at every step . . .

PAY DIRT

Lee Walker

Jim Payne, Sheriff of Cedar Springs, was only delivering his ma's letter to his estranged brother, Michael. Golden Gulch was a dangerous Californian boomtown, in the grip of the ruthless conman Coleridge Craven and his henchman, Kid Cassidy. Jim delivers the letter, but it seems Golden Gulch doesn't want him to go. He must face an old family feud, a miners' revolt and the murderous intentions of Craven and the Kid, if he wants to leave Golden Gulch alive . . .

THE HIRED ACE

Clay Starmer

Trouble is a trade for seasoned gunslinger Reno Valance. When he reaches White Falls, the place seethes and mayhem reigns. With bullets flying, Reno must act. He takes a sheriff's oath and his Remington six-gun — but is it enough? Amidst murder and carnage, evil killers kidnap Anna May, the woman he loves. Can he rescue her and restore order? For two decades he's known victory. Can he prove again that hell is in the hand of The Hired Ace?